THREE NOVELLAS
BY JOHN MANN

Drugs for all reasons

ABSINTHE | DRUGS FOR ALL REASONS | A NEW LIFE

THREE NOVELLAS
BY JOHN MANN

Drugs for all reasons

ABSINTHE | DRUGS FOR ALL REASONS | A NEW LIFE

MEREO
Cirencester

Published by Mereo

Mereo is an imprint of Memoirs Publishing

1A The Wool Market Cirencester Gloucestershire GL7 2PR
info@memoirsbooks.co.uk   www.memoirspublishing.com

DRUGS FOR ALL REASONS

ISBN: 978-1-86151-106-5

Contents

A huge thank you to Chris Newton of Mereo Publishing for his excellent copy editing, and also to my wife, who as usual was my sternest critic!

'There are only three things to be done with a woman: you can love her, suffer for her, or turn her into literature' – Lawrence Durrell, Justine

Jean La Fosse was preparing his third absinthe. He carefully poured iced water over the sugar cube that rested on a perforated spoon, then watched as it trickled through the spoon, turning the liquid in the glass beneath to a milky opacity with a greenish-yellow hue.

His senses were already somewhat dulled, but he had not yet reached the state of morbid introspection that came with the fourth glass. Although seated at a table under a large chestnut tree, he could still feel the force of the early afternoon sun. It was not the dry heat of Provence but the slightly more humid heat of the Jura, and Jean was already beginning to feel uncomfortable. His heavy lunch lay mostly undigested in his belly and the alcohol was starting to make him grumpy - he was certainly not looking forward to returning to the stables of the local château. The job this afternoon was to heave the heavy bales of freshly mown hay up into the loft for storage until needed in the winter months.

This was far removed from his earlier career as a legionnaire in a hot and sand-blown fort in Morocco, where the tedium of long guard duties and senseless parades was relieved by the occasional skirmish with Touareg dissidents. If the days were boring, the nights were even more tedious - and dangerous, too. With no female company, groups of testosterone-loaded males roamed the fort in search of male-on-male sex, and took at knife-point what was not offered freely. This nightly activity was interrupted once a month when a cartload of prostitutes was shipped in for those who would risk possible infection and could afford the excessive prices charged by the women.

There was little else to relieve the boredom - apart from absinthe. The 19th century French armies had grown to love the oblivion provided by the bitter opaque liquor with its flavour of wormwood and hyssop and the alcoholic strength of triple-distilled brandy. During the Napoleonic campaigns in North Africa it had been valued because it kept intestinal worms at bay, but the induction of oblivion was its most endearing and enduring feature.

Out of the corner of his eye Jean spotted a shape he recognised. His wife of ten years was crossing the edge of the square - nothing too unusual about that - except that she was with the village notary, Eustace de Séverin. Florence was ten years younger than Jean and at 25 years she still had a shapely figure, despite bearing him two children. The notary was about her age and known to be a ladies' man, but his wealth and position had thus far kept him clear of retribution from suspicious husbands. Jean rose unsteadily from the table, anger rising within him.

"Hey Jean, you've not finished your absinthe!" It was the owner of the bar - a good personal friend and a drinking companion. Jean returned to the table and downed the contents in one swallow.

"Have another Jean, I've got something to celebrate. You know that shapely little piece at the Café Martin? She's agreed to be my girl. Don't you agree she's got the most beautiful pair of breasts in the village?"

Jean slumped back into the chair he had vacated and the barman prepared him another absinthe.

"You're too bloody fortunate, I've just seen my wife with that womanising notary."

"I thought you two had a good marriage. Why should she be interested in him, don't you keep her satisfied?" The barman gave Jean a playful nudge to the ribs with his elbow. Jean pushed him away angrily.

"Course I bloody do. She gets all she wants - and more besides," scowled Jean.

"Come on, stop fretting, I'm sure she wouldn't cheat on you - let's have another drink and enjoy the sun, " and he poured Jean another absinthe.

* * * * *

The room was home to three postgraduates, Toby, Gaynor and me (Philip), plus an untidy collection of chemicals and glassware, and on three mornings each week, Toby's six-month old baby son. Although termed a research laboratory, the room owed more to the nineteenth-century origins of the building than anything one would associate with a scientific lab in the second half of the twentieth century. The late Victorian aura was reinforced by the antiquated plumbing and the stained mahogany benches and cupboard units that almost filled the room, their variegated markings as much due to numerous chemical spillages as to the patina of age. The baby, Jonathan, seemed happy enough to occupy the bottom drawer of one of the cupboards. His docility was remarked upon by all those who visited the lab, and in hindsight was probably due to the mixture of ether, chloroform and occasionally benzene that permeated the room and his tiny lungs.

Jonathan's mother, Enid, was only part way through a medical degree and the baby was the unscheduled product of a wild birthday celebration. This had culminated in a passionate fling with Toby, while they were under the influence of nitrous oxide, on the operating theatre table of her teaching hospital. Such careless behaviour seems inexcusable in the 21st century, but was common in the mid 1960s when the contraceptive pill was newly available yet required a prescription from the GP and an interview that made the Inquisition seem benevolent. For the male, a furtive expedition to a seedy shop full of trusses, elastic stockings and strange plastic and metal contraptions (what were they for?) was needed. Most buyers went quickly in, looking neither to left or right, mumbled their contraceptive needs to the man in the white coat, and left with equal urgency clutching brown paper bags. Toby and Enid were both good Catholics and had availed themselves of neither of these prophylactic measures, relying instead on a misguided belief in the regularity of the menstrual cycle. The sinful nature of premarital sex had been inculcated by the nuns and Christian Brothers at their respective Catholic secondary schools. Other gems of advice (for girls) had included the necessity for a cushion if you were tempted to sit on an excitable boy's lap, and the need to avoid tampon use for fear of accidental defloration. The Christian Brothers were more to be feared for their brutality and tendency to touch the best endowed boys in the showers.

Toby and Enid had desperately clung to their virginities until they left home and escaped the long reach of their local priests, but soon after they met at university, and at the conclusion of Enid's 18th birthday celebrations, the influence of alcohol, nitrous oxide and years of sexual frustration got the better of them. Despite his unplanned conception, Jonathan was much adored by both his parents and most of those who saw him in his drawer.

The adoration of Jonathan was not quite total. Gaynor viewed him with a curious mixture of maternal desires and wanted to cosset and cuddle him, together with a strong air of disapproval bred of her strict upbringing as the daughter of a Presbyterian minister. She was certainly no prude, and she was quite pretty with her red hair and freckles. This, coupled with her sometimes fiery temperament and general air of disdain where men were concerned, made her an attractive target for the Chemistry Department 'wolves'. On several occasions at drunken birthday revels I had tried to seduce her, but never got beyond a few stolen kisses and the first serious grope. Such approaches were rebuffed firmly but without contempt. Her defloration would, she claimed, require someone more handsome and hunkier than me; but we remained the best of friends.

The presence of a baby in the lab was anathema for our research supervisor, Professor Roger Arbuthnott-Jones - RAJ for short. He could not bring himself to exclude the baby from the lab, for Toby was his favourite student, but as Head of Department he had to exert his authority. His solution was to issue an edict that all laboratory doors should be firmly closed when research was in progress, lest noxious vapours escape and upset the female secretaries, whose olfactory sensitivities to chemical substances were well known. This ensured that visitors would be unlikely to espy Jonathan and report this aberration to higher authorities.

His fears were somewhat irrational, because the activities that took place in his own office were far more likely to occasion comment than a baby in a drawer. For RAJ was a liqueur maker *par excellence*, and his spacious office was crammed with distillation apparatus and glass jars containing a plethora of fruits and plants steeped in absolute alcohol. There were few fruits that had not been macerated and subjected to alcoholic extraction, and the choice was more to do with economics than any desire to produce the ultimate liqueur. For example, on a recent visit to the Windward

Islands, where he was External Examiner for the Chemistry degree courses in the West Indies, he had spotted enormous piles of rotting bananas. Within hours he had arranged for the Geest banana boats to transport not only the main cash crop of the island but also what had hitherto gone to waste. The resultant liqueur smelt like nail varnish but was fantastic with vanilla ice cream.

His latest project involved an attempt to recreate the banned liquor absinthe. When pressed by the Provost, during a recent visit, to explain the impedimenta in his office, this experiment with absinthe provided him with the perfect excuse. All of his research students were, he claimed, working on various aspects of the chemistry or pharmacology of the natural product thujone, the major constituent of the plant wormwood from which absinthe was prepared.

"The trick", RAJ would explain, "is to get the right balance of plants. Pierre Ordinaire died without revealing his original recipe - so we have only the claims of his landlady to go on. God knows what kind of hold she had over him. She claimed, so the books say, to have written down the recipe on several scraps of paper which she sold to Louis Pernod. But I think his secret died with him."

"But how will you know you've made the real thing?" someone would always ask.

"That's easy - Ordinaire's absinthe was the most potent aphrodisiac ever created - of that there is no doubt. All contemporary accounts are unanimous in their enthusiasm for the stuff. The absinthe produced on a huge scale by

Pernod and the other makers in their distilleries never achieved the same star quality, whatever the drunken artists of the time would have us believe."

The next question was always the same - and rather obvious.

"Who will you test it on? Your tutorial group?"

RAJ always ducked the issue of testing, preferring to assure his questioners that he would know instinctively when he had recreated the aphrodisiacal brew.

Despite his recent conversion to the pseudochemical arts, RAJ had had an illustrious scientific career. It was claimed that he was christened plain Roger Jones and had taken his mother's maiden name, Arbuthnott, when the chemical journals began to list the authors of research papers in alphabetical order. But that was probably malicious gossip of the kind that abounds in chemical circles. His research career had begun at University College London, then a centre of excellence for mechanistic organic chemistry, and with Hughes and Ingold as his joint supervisors he could boast, without fear of contradiction, that he had received a world-class education. His illustrious supervisors discerned a rising star, and RAJ was appointed to a Junior Lectureship soon after finishing his Ph.D. research, a not unusual course of events in the 1950s. He rapidly made a name for himself through his studies on steroid biosynthesis, and was the first to propose (correctly as it turned out) the mechanism of a complex rearrangement that still bears his name.. His promotion to Senior Lecturer and then Reader was swift and there were offers of Chairs from several of the new redbrick universities, but he chose to stay in London and eventually accepted the offer of the Chair of Natural Products Chemistry at Empire University where at least his initials were most appropriate.

He never married and became increasingly eccentric, firstly in his dress with brightly-coloured bow ties and food-stained waistcoats, then in his behaviour. I recall being trapped with him at the centre of a zebra crossing outside Empire University, when a cocky young van driver hooted with impatience. RAJ reddened visibly, marched to the van door, wrenched it open and bellowed at the driver, "You impatient little sod! Come and sit on the pavement while your elders and betters use the crossing."

Initially the driver stared at him with defiance, not surprising since RAJ was quite diminutive in stature; but his defiance evaporated when RAJ reached in and dragged the totally bewildered driver from the cab and deposited him unceremoniously at the kerbside. The crossing was then completed, to a cacophony of hoots from other impatient drivers.

As with anyone who has reached the sixth decade of their life without apparent evidence of sexual activity, there was a degree of ribald speculation about RAJ's sexual proclivities. There had once been a temporary awakening of interest with a secretary half his age, but she had merely been skittish and had left precipitately once she perceived the unintended results of her kittenish behaviour. And now there was a third year undergraduate named Sophia, with an ample bosom and pushy GP parents who demanded of their offspring a First or else. A Lower Second was definitely well beyond her reach, but she had recognised a paternal streak in RAJ, and was determined to exploit it. RAJ certainly was unaware that he possessed a fatherly air, and was slightly bemused by this bosomy beauty who sought him out for extra tuition with increasing regularity. Her mini skirts seemed to him to get shorter by the visit and her knitted tops must surely be shrinking each time in the wash. While sexual activity had probably not occurred to either of them, this liaison provided sustenance for the department gossips.

In fact Toby and I were joking about an imagined tryst between RAJ and Sophia, when he entered the lab with a small, youngish, lightly-bearded man reminiscent of the pictures one sees of Toulouse Lautrec.

"This is Professor John Pewsey, our new Professor of Organic Chemistry. These are my three research students, Gaynor, Toby and Philip."

We shook hands in turn - a very painful experience, since he squeezed our hands with a vice-like grip. It occurred to me that here was a man who had been bullied as a child and now seized every opportunity to redress the balance.

We were too academically naive to know anything of the political and nepotistic machinations that had preceded the appointment of Pewsey. He had a reputation nationally for arrogance and self-aggrandisement and had not been the first choice of the department or of the selection panel. But his referees were from Oxbridge, and one was rumoured each year to be on the shortlist for the Nobel prize in Chemistry, though he had obviously made too many enemies ever to reach that particular hall of fame. Even this over-abundance of favourable comment might not have been enough, given his somewhat deficient publication record, had his uncle not been a peer of the realm. A relatively minor peer by all accounts, but very rich and on the boards of several large chemical companies, who had been persuaded to promise several substantial monetary gifts to the department. At interview Pewsey endeared himself to the Provost (but not to his organic chemistry colleagues) by describing these potential colleagues as "a bunch of decrepit old farts, if you'll excuse the expression Provost". Such 'dead wood' would be savagely excised once he was appointed. This was music to the Provost's ears, and when the department's favoured candidate was overly sycophantic to RAJ, not the Provost's favourite Head of Department, he sealed his fate.

"Gentlemen, I don't think we need to discuss anything," the Provost announced once the final candidate had withdrawn. "The choice is quite clear-cut. Can I assume that we will unanimously recommend Dr. Pewsey for the Chair?"

There were sharp intakes of breath around the table, but all the organic chemistry staff were too cowardly to speak – apart from RAJ, who made as if to speak.

"Yes, Professor Jones?" The Provost always left off the 'Arbuthbott' to annoy RAJ.

RAJ sighed disconsolately. "He seems grossly lacking in publications - a jumped-up self-publicist if ever I saw one" he said.

"But at least his research activities seem more mainstream that your own studies with alcoholic beverages," countered the Provost with a sneer.

"But where is the evidence of the world-leading research he brags about?"

The Provost was not to be moved. "Right, that's settled then. I will speak to all of the candidates and let you know how much the Chemistry Department must contribute to the 'dowry'. Good day gentlemen."

RAJ continued with his introductions.

"My group is studying the chemistry of the plant *Artemisia absinthium*."

"Isn't that the one they used to make absinthe?" commented Pewsey perceptively.

"Ah yes - but my students are only interested in the biosynthetic pathways used by the plant to produce natural products."

Pewsey was unconvinced.

"Didn't I hear that you're trying to make the real thing?"

RAJ was on the point of denying this - as he always did - when Jonathan whimpered. For an instant Pewsey looked puzzled, then he darted around the corner of the benching and saw the baby in the drawer. Toby lifted him from his wooden bed and discovered the inevitable wet towelling nappy.

"He needs a change" he said, and laid him back in the drawer while he rummaged around in another set of drawers for a dry nappy.

"This is a bit irregular!" snorted Pewsey. "What about health and safety considerations?"

"Oh - he's perfectly safe - my students don't do anything dangerous," reassured RAJ. "Let me show you the new mass spectrometer."

With that he ushered Pewsey from the lab, but it was clear that the latter's poor opinion of the department had been reinforced and extended.

Of course we did do dangerous things. We distilled hazardous chemicals and solvents in the open lab, for there was no fume cupboard; we manipulated radioactive compounds; and the room was covered in a thin film of the silica we used for chromatography. The 60s were an era free of the restrictions imposed by the later Health and Safety at Work Acts and the highly restricting COSHH regulations. We worked in a lab that had been designed by a physical chemist who believed that organic chemists were a waste of space and were at best technicians who made compounds on which physical chemists could make measurements.

I should explain the avowed aims of our research. We injected small samples of radioactive compounds into cuttings obtained from *Artemisia absinthium* in the hope of following their fate as the plantlets desperately tried to rid themselves of the chemicals through metabolism. My experiments rarely succeeded because I was rather clumsy with the cuttings, and they usually keeled over and died soon after administration of the radiolabelled compounds. I considered this to be rather unsporting of them - giving up the ghost rather than helping with my experiments. Toby and Gaynor were much more skilful and their plants survived the ordeal and yielded results.

I was much better at making things, that is in chemical synthesis, and thus had been given the task of making various structural analogues of thujone. My chromatographic skills were also well developed and the silicaceous dust in the lab arose primarily from my large-scale separations.

We were all, including Jonathan, daily exposed to malodorous and undoubtedly toxic vapours, to the invisible beta-particles from the radiolabelled compounds, and to a dust whose particle size was similar to that which caused silicosis in miners. Others were in greater peril. There was one chemistry building constructed in the 60s that had glass fibre lagging on the *inside* of the air-intake and circulation pipes. As the lagging crumbled with age, the fine silica particles were thus blown around the building and deep into the lungs of the unsuspecting occupants of that department. And yet we thought nothing of our perilous environment. We enjoyed our work, we had fun both inside and outside of the lab, and were grateful to receive the paltry sum of £550 a year from the government.

★ ★ ★ ★ ★

Toby and Enid lived in the attic flat of a dilapidated four-storey Victorian house, in which the other human inhabitants had a colour and variety matched only by the wildlife with which they coexisted. The latter included dry rot, wet rot, woodworm, cockroaches, mice and the occasional rat. The humans were all of the species *Homo sapiens*, but that was the only thing they had in common . They included a Jamaican lady of easy virtue, who lived in the basement and whose calling cards adorned all the local telephone boxes. These described her variously as a 'blow-up dolly', 'pneumatic Primrose', or, more informatively, as 'five-pound Primrose'. A delightful, elderly Mauritian couple lived on the ground floor, and were employed as caretakers and rent collectors. The first floor flat was home to a couple of gay male musicians, who were charming and also very talented. Like Primrose, they slept all morning and were professionally employed at night. Finally, on the floor below Toby and Enid resided an apparently normal, if rather lascivious student from Hong Kong, who claimed to be studying Economics but rarely went to college.

The house would at one time have been the residence of a well-to-do Victorian family, complete with servants' quarters in the attic rooms, with plenty of room for 'below-stairs' activities in the basement. Its location in Westbourne Park Road, just a few streets from the Portobello Road, had once been quite fashionable but had now grown seedy. While Westbourne Park Road still retained a faded air of gentility, the adjoining side-streets, with their flaking facades and crumbling brickwork, were littered with discarded cookers, fridges and sofas, battered cars and the occasional psychedelically-painted VW caravanette.

The flats were mainly occupied by Irish and West Indian families, or so it seemed on a Friday night, when the contents of the weekly paypackets had been spent in the many local pubs. The rhythmic sounds of Rastafarian music and drunken Irish ballads increased in loudness as midnight approached, and the almost inevitable violent climax was usually reached by 2 am on Saturday morning. Some weeks an altercation would be precipitated by the Irish telling the other side to "Foocking shutyer nigra row!", although it was just as likely to emanate from a plea to "Shut yer caterwauling Man and take der next boot back to de bogs!" In any event, the subsequent noise pattern was always the same: a cacophony of raised voices, yells, sounds of broken glass, louder yells (of pain), police sirens, the sound of running feet, and more shouts of "Get yer foocking hands off me, copper!", and finally doors slamming, then absolute silence.

These were the weekly events Toby had just described to the guests at the first 'Wormwood Supper', held in their rather dilapidated and very cold attic flat. The other guests included Deepak, the student from Hong Kong, James, one of the gay musicians, Gaynor, me, and RAJ as guest of honour. He had brought some of his office-produced absinthe as aperitif, and was at that moment pouring water through a perforated spoon bearing a cube of sugar, into several small glasses each containing one ice cube and some absinthe.

"You must now add water to taste - but I recommend three parts for maximum effect" he said.

"What effect?" enquired Deepak, who was ignorant of the alleged properties of the liquor. RAJ enlightened him.

"It was an aphrodisiac, but not without its dangers. To quote Oscar Wilde: *After the first glass you see things as you wish they were. After the second, you see things as they are not. Finally you see things as they really are, and that is the most horrible thing in the world.* Although you might prefer an alternative French description:

Je suis la Fée Verte,
Ma robe est couleur d'esperance,
Je suis la ruine et la douleur,
Je suis le deshonneur,
Je suis la mort,
Je suis l'Absinthe. "

"That sounds like my kind of drink," leered Deepak, draining his first glass. "I'll have another."

"Lascivious creep" retorted Enid. Trapped at home with Jonathan much of the time, she was most familiar with the daily arrivals and departures of girls visiting Deepak. While not over-endowed with good looks, Deepak could, when he liked, exude oriental charm, and with his tales of rich uncles and a fortune to be inherited at 25, he was enormously successful with girls. The fortune was genuine, since his late grandfather had been one of the founders of Hong Kong World Airlines, and had made millions smuggling opium into Hong Kong from Macau. The terms of his will ensured that Deepak received an education in the West - Eton and LSE thus far - but he had to live on a pittance while being educated, so that he would appreciate the wealth when he inherited it at 25. Toby claimed that Deepak spent the pittance on alcohol, cheap Chinese take-aways and condoms.

At a time when air travel had not yet reached the mass

market, Deepak was very well travelled by virtue of his connections with Hong Kong World Airlines. He always carried two passports: a British one, of course, and an Israeli one since his mother was from that country. The latter passport was particularly useful for trips to New York for Christmas shopping - a Jewish origin always seemed to speed his passage through Immigration - but for his diving trips to the Red Sea, the Israeli passport would have been a complete disaster at the Egyptian point of entry, while the British passport (despite the Suez debacle) was still most acceptable along with a little *baksheesh*.

Interesting culinary aromas were emanating from the tiny kitchen.

"Something smells good," commented Gaynor. "Do we have wormwood with every course?"

"Almost" responded Enid. "You can sprinkle dried flowerheads into the soup, and we'll finish with wormwood cake - Dundee cake with dried, crushed leaves in place of the ground almonds."

"Sounds toxic to me" I ventured.

"Or a turn-on" said Deepak. "When can we start?"

Enid brought in the home-made minestrone soup, which was so crammed with vegetables and pasta that there was little room for any liquid. The proximity of Portobello Road ensured a ready supply of cheap fresh vegetables, so although she and Toby lived an impecunious existence, they did at least have a healthy diet. She ladled the thick, nutritious broth into bowls and then produced a small pot containing dried, pulverised and highly aromatic flower heads.

"You can guess what this is. I left out the oregano but you can have some of that if you prefer."

"They smell so, so..." Gaynor searched for the right adjective, which was promptly supplied by Deepak:

"Aphrodisiacal," and he lunged for the bowl with his spoon.

This proved to be a disaster. In his haste to procure the aphrodisiacal plant products, Deepak leant heavily on the edge of the table, forgetting from his previous meals with Toby and Enid that their circular table was in reality a wooden disc balanced on a rickety trellis table. The lack of attachment between disc and trellis meant that heavy downwards pressure had to be avoided. Deepak's bowl of soup slid, as if in slow motion, over the edge and into his lap. He leapt to his feet with a shriek of pain, scalded on both thighs and with what appeared to be someone's entrails slowly sliding down his trousers to the floor. We made a grab for our own bowls and glasses, as they threatened to follow Deepak's bowl in accordance with Newton's Laws. Deepak rushed to the kitchen, seeking cold water and a dish cloth, closely followed by both Enid and Toby. The rest of us, suffering from a mixture of surprise, relief and suppressed laughter, commenced eating to minimise the sense of drama.

The soup was excellent, the wormwood imparting a subtle bitterness to the mass of vegetables and pasta. Toby and Deepak returned. Deepak was without his trousers and wrapped in a dressing gown, looking somewhat pale and deflated, whilst Toby could barely disguise a smirk of satisfaction at seeing a 'loudmouth' humbled. Enid toiled on in the kitchen putting the finishing touches to a minced beef, red kidney bean and chilli concoction. The meals at their place were always basic but very tasty. Toby brought home £550 a year and she received a student grant of £350, so with a weekly rent of seven guineas there was not much left over for luxuries. Regular guests always remembered to bring a packet of chocolate biscuits or a bottle of half-decent wine, since these commodities were rarely present in their flat unless they had just visited Toby's mother, who always sent them home with a box of groceries.

On this occasion RAJ had brought a respectable bottle of claret, while the rest of us had brought those enormous seven-pint cans of beer, Watneys Party 7s. James, the musician, and Deepak worked their way through the beer, while the rest of us feigned sophistication and commented on the 'delicate nose' of the claret, though you certainly couldn't taste it once we started on the main course - a chilli. The alcohol began to work its chemical magic and elevated our moods and loosened our tongues. Toby asked RAJ how he was going to assess the efficacy of his office-brewed absinthe.

"I've obviously considered giving it to my female students" he said, winking at Gaynor. "But since gross moral turpitude is one of the few grounds for dismissal - apart from criminal insanity - I am really at a loss over what to do."

"Why not let Deepak have a bottle or two?" I suggested. " He's the only one of us who is sexually active enough for the effects to be apparent."

"Sounds good to me," Deepak responded. "I could use it weekends and abstain during the week, and then compare my performance."

James was obviously amused. "Since your balls are clearly bigger than your brain, we would at least establish which organ was most affected!"

"At least I use my balls for their proper purpose, " retorted Deepak.

Enid intervened. "Let's have pudding."

The wormwood cake was both an olfactory and gustatory surprise. In appearance it was like a Dundee cake, but this familiarity concealed an intense bitterness and strong herbal aroma. We were variously affected by sensations of mild distaste (Toby and me) or disgust (all of the rest). Deepak was especially affected.

"That is awful!" he spluttered, spitting out a large soggy mass of cake. Enid was obviously disappointed.

"I think I should have put more sugar in it, but Jonathan knocked over the packet and when I went to scoop up the sugar, it had mouse droppings in it. Sorry."

James made an effort to salvage the situation.

"I'm sure it would be great with extra sugar, but have you tried smoking wormwood rather than eating or drinking it? The aroma's a bit like pot."

At that time most of us had not tried pot, but James' lifestyle as musician and homosexual brought him into contact with an array of interesting characters who had access to a variety of illicit commodities, and he began to tell us of his experiences. Most nights he played alto saxophone in a small club called the Green Carnation just off the Bayswater Road. The club provided a mixture of good jazz and blues music combined with an hourly strip show of dubious quality. The strippers were, in most cases, well past their prime and the shows were more titillating - tassels on the ends of nipples waved in the faces of red-faced, paunchy middle-aged men - than sexually arousing. The drinks were grossly over-priced, the entrance charges were outrageous, and for an extra charge, a team of underpaid Asiatic immigrants would knock up a greasy chicken in the basket or a chilli con carne in a kitchen that would have sent a food inspector into a state of apoplexy. It was an open secret that drugs could be obtained, and a number of sharply-dressed and obviously very hard Caribbean men moved from table to table overtly offering purple hearts, cannabis and small squares of blotting paper impregnated with LSD. It was this last commodity that was most highly valued, and a single one centimetre square would cost the purchaser a cool £20.

"I'm sure the acid is made locally." confided James, as we sipped our coffee. "£20 is quite pricey but it's much more than that outside London. I don't suppose any of you guys in the Chemistry Department fancies doing a bit of moonlighting?"

"Now there's a thought," said Toby, "a nice way to supplement a PhD stipend. I wonder how it's done?"

RAJ enlightened us. "Pretty straightforward, the medics use a lot of ergometrine in obstetrics, you just hydrolyse this to make lysergic acid, make the acid chloride and mix it with diethylamine. Anyone with some simple equipment and a bit of chemical knowledge could do it."

"So why don't you make some, instead of mucking around with absinthe?" opined Deepak.

"Because I like my creature comforts too much and don't fancy the damp and cold of Wormwood Scrubs."

At that point further discussion was rendered impossible, as the one gas fire in the flat spluttered and died.

"It does this every evening," explained Toby. "Somewhere in the building a vast gust of air gets into the gas pipe and the whole system sucks back."

"So that lets you all off the hook as regards washing up," announced Enid, "because there won't be any hot water until the morning. I bet you're all really devastated."

We all apologised for not being able to help, thanked them both for their hospitality, and stumbled down the stairs and into the night air. RAJ gave Gaynor and me a lift back to her hall of residence, which was just a few roads from my flat. The alcohol had obviously had a more substantial effect on Gaynor than I had realised, because she suddenly threw her arms round my neck and gave me a very full kiss, her small tongue darting around in my mouth. Given my previous lack of success in trying to seduce her, this was a real surprise.

"D'you want to come in for a bit?"

"I didn't think that was possible - the porter would never let me through the door at this time of night." Like all female halls of residence in the sixties, Gaynor's was a veritable virgins' retreat - certainly after nightfall.

"I'll open the window and you can climb in."

Gaynor's room was on the ground floor round at the side of the building, so this was technically feasible, though as I discovered several minutes later, there were vertical bars on the window designed to keep rampant males out of the building. I was certainly feeling pretty rampant by now and keen to breach these defences. There is nothing better to get the juices going than to be asked into the bedroom of the female you have lusted after for several months. I even had my trusty packet of three with me. Indeed I had been an optimistic condom carrier since I was thirteen, but was not one of Nature's great seducers, so the packet and contents were now well out-of-date.

Somehow I managed to squirm through the bars, and without further preliminaries we began to snog on Gaynor's bed. Like any hot-blooded lad I knew things had to progress, and after a few minutes of rolling and hip thrusting, my hand made a dart up the front of Gaynor's jumper. I was delighted when she made no attempt to remove my hand from her right bra cup. Emboldened, I decided it was time to make a play for removal of the bra. Always a tricky manoeuvre, since you had to make sure your lips remained firmly engaged and tongues intertwined while your brain was desperately trying to work out how to undo the various clasps and fastenings.

I had finally wrenched it free with a tiny whoop of triumph when there was a loud thumping on the door. I had read in books about a 'heart-stopping' moment, and now I knew what they meant. We both froze, our hearts pounding away in unison.

"Are you in there Miss MacEnery?"

More thumping. Gaynor affirmed her presence in a squeaky, barely audible voice.

"Someone has reported seeing an intruder entering the building on this side. Can I come in?"

I had to give Gaynor her due, her alcohol-befuddled brain suddenly functioned with utmost clarity.

"Quick - under the bed," she hissed in my ear, and I certainly needed no second bidding. I was under the bed with her suitcase, fluffy slippers and assorted heaps of dust faster than I could ever remember moving before.

"Just a moment, I'm getting my dressing gown."

The door was unlocked and the warden or whoever it was came into the room. Her large black brogues and brown, wrinkled stockings came and stood within an inch of my nose - a nose that was already beginning to fill with dust and dust mites, and would not be restrained from sneezing indefinitely.

"You seem to be all right - let me know if you see or hear anything suspicious."

"Of course, Miss Wainwright."

"And you must tidy this room – a floor covered with discarded underwear and food wrappers is not acceptable."

And she was gone. My loudly thumping heart began to slow and I wriggled out from under the bed, and immediately sneezed loudly.

"Shoosh, she'll hear you."

"Sorry."

I put my arm around her waist and pulled her towards me,

ready and eager to carry on where we had left off. She pushed me away firmly.

"No - you can't stay. Let me see if the coast is clear."

She opened the window and peered out. The alley seemed to be quiet, so with one final hurried snog, I was propelled out into the night with mixed emotions. On the one hand there was the triumph of removing Gaynor's bra, and on the other, that gut-clenching hand of fear for what could have been a very nasty situation. Something to brag about in the pub anyway.

* * * * *

In common with 25 million other Britons, I spent much of the next day watching the funeral of Winston Churchill. He had fallen ill soon after his 90th birthday in November 1964, and his slow progress towards death was mirrored by the ever-increasing gloom on the face of his physician Lord Moran as he read his daily bulletins. The slowness of the progression had caused not a little financial difficulty for the daily papers as they composed and then re-composed their first editions each night, but finally on January 24th, he had slipped away and this event precipitated an outburst of national mourning not seen since Horatio Nelson arrived back from the Battle of Trafalgar pickled in a cask of rum. Now, six days later, I was clinging to the top of a wire fence trying to get a view of the courtyard of St. Paul's Cathedral. I had distant views of the serried ranks of military groups, led by a small contingent of Battle of Britain pilots - a few of 'The Few' - and those other groups like the Fire Brigade and Civil Defence who had been so much part of England's Finest Hour. I could see the host of kings and queens, presidents and prime ministers as they filed into the cathedral, but couldn't see who they were. The papers later reported that more of the great and the good had been there than had been at that other great funeral of the 60s, that of JFK. Here were two men who in life had had influence over the lives and destinies of much of the World's population. American presidents would unfortunately continue to wield that sort of power, but Churchill was to be the last Briton to do so.

After the service, I surged with the crowd towards the river, and saw the launch carry his body towards Waterloo Pier for its onward journey by rail to Bladon. The rows of cranes in the London docks all lowered their jibs as the launch passed by, and the poignancy of this act brought tears to my eyes. I fought them back, surprised by my emotions, for while Churchill had been a hero to my parents, he had only been a character in a serial on the back-page of *The Eagle* for me.

I turned away from this outpouring of emotion and wandered back towards my flat in Camden Town. Everything was shut - shops, cinemas, museums, schools and colleges - but I was surprised to find that the library of our college was open, and thinking that Gaynor might be inside, I went in. She was a bit of a swot and often spent her spare time reading the current chemical journals. In fact, we relied on her to keep us informed about new and relevant research. She wasn't around, but the library was warm and had a decent coffee machine, and I suddenly had a hankering to find out about absinthe.

Three hours later, like RAJ, I was hooked on the subject.

I had always believed that absinthe was the drink of the artisans and literati of 19th century Paris - the Montmartre set - and so it was. But what I had not appreciated was the huge annual consumption of absinthe by the French, rising from 70,000 litres in 1875 to more than 35 million litres in 1910. Not surprisingly there was a high degree of alcoholism associated with a drink that was made from triply distilled brandy and herbal essences, and this was often associated with a condition that became known as *absinthism*. The pale and mentally-enfeebled creatures you see in the paintings of the time who were suffering from this condition usually ended their days in asylums or committed suicide; in fact concern for the rising numbers of its citizens suffering in this way led the French government to ban absinthe in 1915. Countries like Switzerland and Belgium had banned the drink four years earlier, following several well-publicised court cases involving murders perpetrated by habitual absinthe drinkers. But that was only the tail end of the story of absinthe. Its origins were just as fascinating.

In biblical times, a concoction made from leaves of wormwood (*Artemisia absinthium*) suspended in wine or spirits was used as a treatment for stomach problems, jaundice, rheumatism, halitosis, and to alleviate the pain of childhood. St. John in his *Revelations* mentions that "the third part of the waters became wormwood: and many men died of the waters, because they were made bitter" - a dire warning of the effects of absinthism perhaps. Throughout the Middle Ages, various extracts of wormwood were use as stomach purges and cures for flatulence, and the great 18th century herbalist Nicholas Culpeper extolled its virtues to combat the "evils of Venus" and to stem the "wanton boy produce" - whatever that was. There may even have been something resembling absinthe in Elizabethan England, since various brews were made from dried leaves of wormwood steeped in malmsey wine and then 'thrice distilled'. The *purl* of this period was made from a mixture of ale and wormwood, and must have tasted ghastly.

The modern history of absinthe began in 1792, when the appropriately named Pierre Ordinaire first began to market his *La Fée Verte* in the small village of Couvet in Switzerland. Actually, the various books 'squabbled' over whether Ordinaire or a pair of sisters called Henriod were the first to prepare absinthe. What they agreed about was that the recipe involved wormwood, anise and varying amounts of hyssop, coriander, camomile, and other herbs. These were all steeped in strong brandy for a about a week, and then the concoction was distilled. Initially the absinthe was sold purely for medicinal purposes, until 1797 when a Major Henri Dubied found that the drink was not only good for his indigestion, chills and bronchial problems, but also helped his sexual performance. The future of absinthe was thus assured, and Dubied bought the recipe from the Henriod sisters and set up his distillery in Couvet in partnership with his daughter's new husband, a fellow called Henri-Louis Pernod. This man's name was, of course, destined to be forever associated with anise-flavoured drinks, and in 1805 he split from Dubied to set up his own distillery in Pontarlier in France, trading under the name of Pernod fils.

Eventually I could take no more. My head was spinning with all this new found knowledge, and I had an urge to tell someone about what I had discovered. I used the call-box in the library to phone Gaynor, hoping she'd agree to meet me for a coffee, but her response was far from encouraging.

"You've got a cheek calling me - I was drunk last night and you tried to take advantage of me. I'd have been in terrible trouble if they'd have found you in my room!"

All of which was perfectly true, though I was somewhat peeved that I was being blamed for an act of bravado she had initiated.

"Hey that's unfair - you were the one who invited me into the room."

"Well I don't recall. Anyway I've got far too much to do to come out for a coffee. See you tomorrow." And with that she put the receiver down.

The buzz of sexual excitement that I had felt on the previous evening was obviously not to be repeated - or at least not in the short term. It never failed to amaze me how a girl's mood could swing from day to day. The influence of their hormones I could just about comprehend, but when alcohol was added to the equation the results were totally unpredictable. I packed up all my papers and jottings and headed for the flat.

Camden Town was amazingly quiet, and I was at least a hundred yards from our small basement flat when I heard the unmistakable melody of the Beatles' *Hard Days Night* accompanied by the definitely unmelodic guitar strumming of my flatmate Hugh. He was a chemistry postgrad like me, but worked on gas phase kinetics, which required very little actual experimentation but lots of number crunching. He had been torturing the strings of a Fender guitar, but since he had never bothered to take any lessons, he had barely progressed beyond a few basic chords and some plucking. His other claim to fame was that his feet would put an over-ripe Camembert cheese to shame, and although he changed his socks at least three times a day and the cast-offs were immediately soaked in the newly available Biotex, the flat always retained an effluvium of smelly feet. Fortunately, we each had our own bedroom, so it was possible to make a partial escape.

Hugh was sitting in the communal living room, strumming and humming completely out of tune, as the Beatles sang their hearts out in the background. All of that was absolutely normal, but there was something distinctly odd about the room. It was tidy! The usual piles of old newspapers, toast crumbs, lumps of marmalade and discarded coffee cups with cold, grey contents, were nowhere to be seen. The room had been blitzed.

"You've been busy - quite out of character. Is your Mum coming round or something?"

He stopped strumming. "What you on about?"

"The room - it's brilliant."

"Oh that. Nothing to do with me. One of Cath's fellow student nurses, Alice, needed some cash, so she's going to char for us once a week."

Cath was the long-time girlfriend of my other flatmate, Roland (Roly for short), who was trying to complete his accountancy articles. He had failed the final exam three times already, and retook it at six-month intervals. Cath was in the first year of her SRN training at University College Hospital, and had more or less moved in with Roly.

"Where is this angel of mercy?"

Hugh had returned to his strumming, but motioned in the direction of the kitchen:

"I think she's trying to find the kitchen under all that grease and unwashed crockery."

Like most students, we never washed up until we needed the stuff for cooking in or eating off. Poor girl. But at that moment she appeared in the doorway.

"I've had enough for today - but I've done the washing-up - I'll attack the cooker next week."

Hugh barely stopped strumming long enough to say "thank you" before asking me if I would pay her.

"I've agreed to pay Alice £1 a week and as much coffee and Beatles' music as she can take. I'm skint - can you pay her?"

Pay her - I wanted to hug her! She was gorgeous. If Tenniel had come into the room at that moment, he would surely have recognised his most famous artistic creation. With her flowing blonde locks, delicate features, and blue dress with tight bodice framing her shapely bosom, Alice *was* Alice.

"Yes, I'll pay you - and give you a lift home if you like."

"That would be great, I'm on duty again at 4.30. If I go now, I can get some dinner before work."

The van was outside - my pride and joy, a royal blue Austin A35 van. In those days, if you took the driving test in a van, you did not have to reverse round corners and various other stupid manoeuvres which led to failure and misery for many test candidates. The top speed was a dizzying 55 mph, but she did about 50 to the gallon, so she was ridiculously cheap to run.

"Is this it?" was Alice's response when she saw it.

"Fraid so - would you rather take the tube?"

"No, it's rather sweet."

We set off along the Euston Road towards Gower Street and University College Hospital.

"Do you know where the nurses' home is? Our 'virgins' retreat'."

I laughed - another buzz of sexual excitement. "I can't imagine there are too many of you left in these permissive sixties."

She was not going to be drawn on that and simply laughed. "You'd be surprised. You turn right here, then first left into Huntley Street."

I followed her instructions and we arrived outside a rather severe red brick building attached to the main hospital.

"No man has ever got beyond the ground floor sitting room - not even into the adjacent TV room" she said. She opened the door to get out.

"Can I take you out for a meal some time?"

I couldn't believe my lips were moving.

"OK, that'd be nice. I'm on a straight tomorrow and get off at about 5.30."

"Great - I'll come for you at six."

"Fine- see you then. Bye."

And she was gone - into the forbidden recesses of the nurses' home. Oh to be the first male to storm that bastion!

★ ★ ★ ★ ★

Major Henri Dubied was suddenly aware that he was fighting for breath. The flaccid upper arm of the whore beside him lay across his nose and mouth - the effluvia of stale sweat from her abundant underarm hair filled his nostrils. With a shudder of realisation he pushed her arm roughly aside. She had seemed irresistible after three glasses of *extrait d'herbes medicinales,* and his performance had certainly surprised him. His recent short, perfunctory sexual encounters with his wife had been a disappointment to both of them, but his balls still ached from his night-long copulations with the whore. The bar-room gossip about the *extrait* was evidently well-founded.

The whore snorted in her sleep. Henri Dubied looked over at her – in the morning light she seemed fat and ugly. Should he wake her for a final fling? The ache in his testicles intensified as the idea caused his penis to stir. No, maybe not. At his age, enough was enough.

He eased his considerable bulk out of bed. Where were his

clothes? Discarded all around the room during the half-remembered frenetic activities of the previous evening. He located his voluminous under garments, his long white shirt, pantaloons, waistcoat - even his top hat and frock coat - and began to dress. He was now aware that his head was banging and a tight band seemed to be drawn across his temples. Was it three or four *extraits* he had consumed? He thought it was three, and perhaps one cognac - or was it two cognacs? The whore was still oblivious to the fact that her customer was leaving, but Henri Dubied was an honest man and as he left, he placed two gold napoleons on the table.

A few hours later he sat outside the Bar de la Paix with Henri-Louis Pernod. This had become a regular Friday lunchtime meeting since Pernod had become engaged to Dubied's daughter a year before.

"Louis - you must tell me where you obtain the *extrait d'herbes medicinales* - it has improved my vigour enormously. I am no longer breathless in the morning."

Some intimate secrets could not be shared, especially with a future son-in-law. But Louis was not fooled and was certainly not in any way deferential to Henri, who he considered to be something of a buffoon.

"That's a novel euphemism you old rascal - 'breathless in the morning. But to answer your question, the *extrait* is made by the Henriod sisters - you know - the ones who taught dear Hélène to play the piano and sing."

"Really? They always seemed such simple souls - talented teachers but hardly amateur apothecaries."

For a few minutes they ate in silence, savouring their *salades de chèvre chauds*. Henri eventually made the fateful suggestion.

"Do you think they could be persuaded to tell us how they make it?"

"*Mon Dieu* - you really have been bowled over by the stuff!"

"Well yes - but the point is that others will want to share the secret, and your distillery could provide the spirit which I'm sure forms the base of the *extrait*."

Louis Pernod was an astute businessman who had also experienced the benefits of the *extrait*, so he needed little persuasion. His distillery was profitable, with a limited line of brandies and *eaux de vie*, but this new product was appealing.

Early that same evening, Henri Dubied donned his best suit and visited the sisters Henriod. The sisters were spinsters in their sixties - one taught the piano and harmonium, and the other gave instruction in singing and poetry. Both were small-boned and slight and had long grey hair, severely coiled into tight buns, and wore long black dresses buttoned to the chin. They had no experience of men and neither feared them or disdained them.

Henri was welcomed into the drawing room and offered a small glass of red wine, though they themselves did not partake. The cottage was cluttered with shabby furniture and many ceramic objects, especially jugs, adorned the shelves. After answering polite enquiries after the health of his wife and daughter, Henri moved the conversation in the desired direction.

"My good ladies, I have recently benefited from your

delightful *extrait d'herbes medicinales.* My breathing is greatly improved and my stomach more settled."

They nodded in approval. He continued: "Have you ever considered making your preparation available on a more commercial basis?"

"Why no, Major Dubied," confirmed Henriod senior. "The *extrait* has been in our family for several generations and save for the claims for its modest medicinal benefit, we have never thought it to have any commercial value."

The other sister interjected.

"One of our nephews – a Pierre Ordinaire – did try to sell bottles of the *extrait* some years ago, but he had a rather unfortunate accident."

Henri showed interest:

"May I enquire what happened?"

The sisters looked gravely at one another.

"The poor man was distilling his crude extract when his still exploded," explained the younger Henriod.

"He lost a hand," added the other sister," and the black rot set in. He died in terrible agony."

There was a moment's silence, then Henri made his offer.

"As you know, my future son-in-law Louis Pernod has a small distillery, and he could provide the spirit base that is undoubtedly essential for your *extrait*. There could be a substantial income for you from the sales."

The sisters turned to one another, and with beatific smiles, nodded their agreement.

"It could be a major contribution to human health and

well-being," the Major assured them. And with a totally unrealised irony, Henriod senior said:

"We will be so happy if it will strengthen the members of this village."

★ ★ ★ ★ ★

The next day marked the beginning of a major upheaval for us and our supervisor RAJ. We had just joined the people in the large lab opposite for morning coffee. It had been my turn to supply the communal biscuits and I was handing these around when our new Professor of Organic Chemistry, Prof Pewsey, marched in, bristling with self-importance.

"Who are the ones who work in A23?" he demanded.

Gaynor, Toby and I exchanged glances before acknowledging that we did.

"Well you'll have to move out before the end of the week - I need it for my research."

"But Professor Arbuthnott-Jones hasn't said anything to us," began Gaynor, but she was promptly overwhelmed by Pewsey.

"Your research is not important enough to justify the space - you will have to move into this lab" he said. He stopped short of reminding us that he was Head of the Organic Chemistry Section and that his research was world-class, but that was the message he had been disseminating since his arrival in the Department.

"There's no space in this lab for us," I pointed out.

"You find space to hang around drinking coffee and gossiping. Move some of these chairs out, and there'll be plenty of space. I want you out of A23 by the end of the week."

And with that he turned on his heel and was gone - a small, bearded bully with an ego twice his size.

"What a bastard!" Gaynor was first to give vent to her feelings.

"Jumped-up little prick", was Toby's contribution, but all I could think of was the huge clearance problem presented by years of accumulated junk and bottles of radioactive residues that lay festering in the recesses of A23's cupboards and drawers.

Two members of the 'coffee club' worked for Pewsey, and they seemed as surprised as we were by the turn of events.

"What's the little creep up to Juan?" I asked the paunchy and bearded Spanish postdoc who was trying to prepare an exotic natural product called pongoene for Pewsey.

"Eez a meestery to mee, Fileep."

"Perhaps he's going to lock you away in there Juan," volunteered Peter Sharpfoot, another of Pewsey's group, and we all smirked. The compound pongoene was aptly named. It was derived from a rare plant native to the rain forests of Java which only flowered every five years, but when it did the carrion-like odour of pongoene could be smelt for miles around. Juan had already been thrown out of many of the pubs and coffee bars in the vicinity because his clothes always stank of the chemical intermediates that he was using to prepare it.

People began to drift away back to their experiments, and we three returned gloomily to A23, our cramped, squalid little room. None of us spoke, but we were all thinking much the same things. Giving up a lab with its almost total lack of facilities and strong aroma of terpenes was no big deal, but giving it up to a little shit like Pewsey was annoying. And where would Jonathan sleep?

We had barely begun to contemplate where to begin when an angry exchange of voices reached us from the corridor.

"How dare you presume to take control of my lab without consulting me!"

RAJ had obviously heard the news.

"Don't you raise your voice to me Professor Jones!" Pewsey loved to remind RAJ that he was really only a hyphenated Jones. "You may be Head of Department but I am Head of the Organic Section and I need the space."

"Anyone with an ounce of decency would have discussed the matter with me first."

"I called on you at nine this morning, but your secretary said you were getting some demijohns from the wine-making shop. Jones, your research is a joke and doesn't warrant any space in this Department!"

"You don't occupy much space, you jumped up, self-satisfied little man," fumed RAJ, "but even those few cubic inches are an over-generous provision in this department! You can expect a major cut to your research budget!"

And with that he stormed off, leaving us to begin the task of clearing the lab. In the event it proved to be less tedious than we had anticipated, because the deeper recesses of the cupboards and drawers revealed some amusing and dangerous objects. In a previous existence the lab had been used by one of the early pioneers of organo-lithium chemistry. These substances have a tendency to catch fire spontaneously in the air, as Gaynor discovered when she removed the muck-encrusted stopper from a dusty old flask. There was a whoosh as a jet of flame shot from the mouth of the flask, followed by a squeak from Gaynor and a crash as she threw the flask and contents into the sink. The contents immediately caught fire and for a few seconds the sink was a raging inferno and acrid fumes filled the lab; but it was all over almost as quickly as it had started. This was just as well, because we had used up the contents of the lab CO_2 extinguisher on a previous fire which had threatened Jonathan as he lay in his drawer.

We proceeded with much more caution after that, suspicious even of a grossly fermented and half-consumed tin of Heinz baked beans and a very flat bottle of Coke. The other suspect flasks and bottles we took to the back of the building and hurled bricks at, but only one caught fire and one produced a small detonation and an accompanying puff of acrid smoke. The College Beadle, resplendent in maroon uniform, discovered us at our brick throwing, but was completely unfazed when we explained what we were doing. His job was to look out for student pranksters and Vietnam protesters, and since we were hurling bricks at bottles rather than professors, he was disinclined to get involved.

"Just you clear up your mess - can't have all this glass littering up the place," was his only instruction.

Having disposed of other people's leftovers, we began to dismantle our apparatus and move our glassware and chemicals. Gaynor had her large flasks of agar with clumps of plant cells growing on them - you could spot the successful experiments because they were the ones without green shoots and hence photosynthesis and merely comprised unexciting clumps of brown, undifferentiated cells. Toby had dozens of small flasks full of half-completed reactions - he was very industrious and would always have at least a dozen reactions on the go at any one time. I had my home-made irradiation apparatus: a cardboard box, quartz reaction vessel and mercury lamp. We all possessed lots of radioactive samples, but most of these were in a special lab upstairs.

Toby finished moving his stuff and then went home complaining of a sore throat which he'd had for days and was getting him down. He had also been moaning about a stiff neck all morning. His knees had been bad earlier in the week and he had sought medical help at the Student Health Centre, but the GP had been less than sympathetic and had diagnosed a clear case of student hypochondria.

Gaynor and I were just clearing the last few pots when Pewsey's postdoc, Peter Sharpfoot, arrived to take vacant possession. He was a relative newcomer to the department - a graduate of Harrow and then Exeter whose father was said to be a Professor of Chemistry at a redbrick university. Sharpfoot was thin and weedy-looking, and his wispy hair and thin moustache made him look the geek he surely was.

"Are you nearly done? Professor Pewsey has just told me

I am to have this lab, and I've got lots of equipment to move in" he said. His nasal yet refined voice made his request even more irritating.

"What's this project that is so important?" I enquired, only half-interested.

"It's a new alkaloid with highly interesting biological properties."

"So why does that require the use of *our* lab?"

"Prof. Pewsey says it's important that the work is done in a small lab where I won't be disturbed."

"We can certainly guarantee that!" snorted Gaynor, and pushed past him carrying her last few culture dishes.

"Is it right that you've had a baby in this lab?" Sharpfoot asked.

"Once or twice."

"Well I think it's weird - and so does Prof. Pewsey - he says your Prof. should be booted out."

"Quite frankly I couldn't give a toss what either of you think," I retorted, and with a sneer, "I hope you'll be truly happy in our lab." I brushed past him with my photolysis apparatus and deposited it with all our other junk in the lab opposite.

Gaynor was poking around with her displaced glassware and looking very morose. We had all missed lunch and I suggested going over to the Students' Union for tea and a sandwich, but I was obviously still out of favour following my attempt to 'seduce' her, because she dismissed my suggestion unambiguously:

"I'm pissed off and going home. Sod the lot of you!"

I had a couple of hours to kill before my date with Alice, so I had tea and a bun in the Students' Union. My attempts to complete the unsolved cryptic clues in the crossword of a discarded *Daily Telegraph* were futile as usual, apart from a couple of anagrams. I wandered round to Huntley Street for about six o'clock. The dragon on the door, in what could easily have passed for a sentry box, allowed me entry to the sitting room of the Nurses' Home, then announced my arrival over the tannoy: "Visitor for Nurse Bolton."

Alice appeared almost immediately, already dressed for going out.

"I was just about to give up on you and go out" she said.

"You did say you'd not be ready until six?"

"Oh - we had a quiet day and sister let us off early. Come on then, no time to waste, shall we do some window shopping along Oxford Street? Though I'm stony broke till payday."

We headed off down Tottenham Court Road in the direction of Oxford Street, and I tried to find out a bit more about her job. She was in the first year of her SRN course and had not yet gone beyond the skivvy stage: emptying bedpans, changing beds, washing patients and serving meals. But she was still expected to assist with the laying out of corpses and dispensing drugs - all for a measly seven pounds ten shillings a week, half of which disappeared on board and lodging. As a relatively naive 22-year-old, it all seemed rather tough to me, but 40 years on many things have not changed. The pay is still poor and the responsibilities huge, and it is still nurses rather than doctors who make patients better with their tender loving care.

"Why on earth did you choose to be a nurse and not take the easy option of being a student?" I asked.

"My parents wanted me to go to university, but I couldn't wait to leave school after 'O' Levels. I hated the uniform, homework, sucking up to teachers and having to hang from the wall-bars while the lesbian PE teacher tried to look up your gym knickers."

"We had that kind of stuff too, though our PE teacher flicked you with a towel as you ran through the showers and made the well-endowed boys go through twice so he could get a better look."

We were by now halfway between Tottenham Court Road tube station and Oxford Circus, and then as now, this seedier end of Oxford Street was full of pavement vendors selling cheap jewellery, replicas of London buses and taxis and Union Jack tea towels. But in addition, given that it was the time of Flower Power, the stalls were also loaded with hippy beads, bells and multi-coloured Indian scarves. Alice stopped every so often to finger this merchandise. She seemed particularly taken by the bells threaded onto leather thongs with their high-pitched tinkling sounds.

"Can you lend me five shillings for a bell?" she enquired.

"I'll buy us both a bell, " I suggested and handed a ten shilling note to the scruffy, long-haired vendor, who was himself festooned with beads and bells and wrapped in a fairly lurid kaftan.

"Peace Brother," was his only response, and we tinkled off towards Oxford Circus.

"What did you do after you left school?" I asked her.

"My dad got me a job as a clerk in an insurance office, but it was really deadly and the office boys were real nerds - always leering at me and trying to squeeze me into the Gestetner room. Then one day the boss called me in and told me I was a fool and too intelligent to be working in a dead-end job. He persuaded me to go to the local college and get some 'A' Levels. Funny how you will take advice from someone you don't really know but completely disregard anything your parents tell you."

"That's called being a teenager! So what 'A' Levels did you take?"

"Oh just English and French - I was never any good at science subjects, and they were always such hard work too. So we had to read loads of stuff I wanted to read anyway - you know, *Pride and Prejudice* and *King Lear* - and we also had this gorgeous male English teacher just out of college who made us look at more modern stuff as well - *Catch 22* and *The Ginger Man*, and D H Lawrence's poems etc."

"We did several of his novels for 'O' Level, but I've never read his poems."

"They're really good - full of sexual undercurrents. In fact, that's what our teacher seemed to like about them and he encouraged us to think about sexuality. We all had a crush on him."

I was reminded of one of our teachers.

"Sounds like my 'O' Level English teacher. He'd always be going on about some pretty girl he'd seen at the bus stop that morning and how her face had stayed imprinted on his brain all day. He said it was the same kind of thing that the poets were always rambling on about, but we just had him down as a dirty old man."

"So what about you?" asked Alice. "Why did you want to study Chemistry?"

"Oh you know, the usual. We had a really inspiring teacher in the second year."

But it had been much more than that. I loved the smells of chemistry, the fizzing of the reactions, the unexpected combustions and small explosions in the lab. The more daring (and stupid) exploits that involved squirting flammable solvents onto the labcoats of unsuspecting geeky boys, and then setting them alight. Or the illicit generation of hydrogen sulphide and leading the gas by a tube out of the lab window and into the path of the school cadet force as they marched and wheeled in the playground outside. Better still, the ease of buying chlorate weedkiller and sulphur from the chemist's shop, so that home-made 'gunpowder' was so accessible. The experiments in my father's Anderson shelter at the bottom of our garden, and the unexplained fire in the middle of the night when an unfinished experiment spontaneously combusted. All of this I explained to Alice, but I don't think she was much interested – chemistry is such a turn-off for most people.

We turned into Regent Street and then into Carnaby Street, with its boutiques crammed with pop souvenirs and mod clothes. The street was crowded with evening shoppers, most of whom like us were ogling the weird assortment of psychedelic clothes and the pseudo-military uniforms (complete with those great big 'clothes-brush'-style epaulettes) that were all the rage at the time. I guess most people also went along Carnaby Street hoping to see the odd pop group or two. I never did, though Alice claimed to have seen the Yardbirds and Eric Clapton, then in Cream. We certainly saw no one famous that evening, but we did run into some of her friends.

"Hey you guys," boomed an American voice, "over here!"

We turned to trace the voice and saw two girls waving like mad on the opposite pavement. Both were wearing knee-high leather boots, black and white patterned Mary Quant style minis and white fake fur jackets. One was relatively dumpy, though still skinny by American standards, and the other was plain skinny.

"These are my impossibly rich American friends," Alice hissed under her breath. "They share a flat with some of the girls in the set above mine."

"Hi there Alice - aren't you going to introdoose us to your cute friend?"

"Carol and Carly, this is Philip."

"Great to know you Phil' said Carly, the skinny one. 'Say, you guys doin' anything this evening? Because we're just off back to our place to have some turkey and this jug of wine." Carly indicated a litre bottle of white wine which she was lugging around in a carrier bag,

"What's the celebration?" enquired Alice.

"Who needs a celebration - it's Friday tomorrow for Crissake!"

Alice looked at me and I shrugged to say that I was easy one way or the other.

"OK - that sounds great - can we bring anything?"

Carol and Carly looked at one another.

"I guess we're real short of glasses. Can you guys get hold of some?" asked Carly.

"We can get some from my place," I volunteered. "And at the same time I can pick up my van and give us all a lift to your place."

"Sounds great to me," Carol enthused. "Have you guys finished your shopping?"

We nodded and Alice tinkled her bell. "We just came for some hippy bells" she said.

"Oh they're so neat," oozed Carol, "so ethnic." And with that we headed through the crush for Oxford Circus tube station and thence to Warren Street and my van parked in Gordon Square. Not surprisingly the girls found this tiny, windowless conveyance on four small wheels to be 'neat'.

"Oh gee, we can't all get in that, can we?" wondered Carol; but we did, together with the demijohn of wine and various assorted carrier bags of groceries that the American girls had in tow. The traffic was quite light, so we made good time to Camden town and my flat. Both flatmates were out, presumably with their respective girlfriends. The American girls were obviously a little taken aback by the squalor of our basement flat.

"Gee don't you guys ever wash up?" wondered Carol eyeing the lunch plates with their remnants of baked beans and ketchup and the lump of marmalade adhering to the edge of the table.

Alice was also disturbed. " I was only here yesterday! You boys really know how to mess up a place quickly."

"Alice chars for us once a week, " I explained somewhat meekly.

"What is 'chars' - does she put out for you or something?" from a querulous Carly.

Alice exploded: "No I bloody don't - they pay me to clean this festering hole for them."

"You skivvy for them?" an even more querulous Carly. "But you're a nurse for Crissake."

"Yes - a very poorly paid and over-worked nurse."

I could see this dragging on for some time so I hurried into the kitchen, grabbed some glasses, stuffed them into a Sainsbury's bag and returned to the girls, still in heated debate about filthy students and hard-up nurses, and announced that we could go.

The drive up the Finchley Road was a bit tortuous as we got caught up in the tail-end of the evening rush, but we eventually turned off into a quiet side-street more or less opposite Westfield College, a prime piece of real estate since sold off to the developers. The American girls lived in what must have been a superb family residence in late Victorian times, and like us had the basement rooms. I could see why they were surprised by the squalor of our place, since these rooms were very neat and the furniture was not scarred or scuffed or covered in marmalade. The walls were covered with the usual sixties posters: Che Guevara, some Toulouse Lautrec pictures, various pop stars and travel posters, but also some I hadn't seen before, most of them extolling the virtues of cannabis or LSD.

"Make yourself at home Philip,- you too Alice, " urged Carol, beginning to unload the groceries while Carly busied herself slicing the turkey carcass. "I guess you need some ice for that wine?"

"Yeah, it would be better chilled - have you got a bucket?"

"No, but we've got a very large chamber pot - isn't that what you Brits call it?" and with a flourish she produced the biggest pot I had ever seen, complete with floral designs.

"Sure, that'll be great - have you got some ice cubes?"

"Boy where have you been? Americans don't use 'ice cubes' from cute little trays, we have real fridges and ice dispensers." And she opened the door of the fridge to reveal a dispenser. She pulled a lever and ice cascaded into the po.

"Cool eh?"

I had to admit it was cool in every respect. My view that Americans were always light years ahead of Europeans in the gadgets race was further strengthened. Everything was always bigger, better, and brasher, but yet they were struggling in Vietnam. Just that day, Lyndon Johnson had called on Congress for permission to send more combat troops to the region.

"I bet you girls are glad you're not fellahs and might be sent off to Vietnam any day" I said. Carol and Carly were busy at the stove and chopping board respectively. Carly paused momentarily from her chopping.

"I've already lost a cousin and a boy from my High School class. Goddam Kooks and Johnson." She resumed her chopping with renewed vigour.

"I'm sorry - it's a terrible waste of lives and money."

"Not according to our Government, who believe in the domino effect and the Commie desire for world domination," interjected Carol. "We've been on all the peace marches, waved our banners outside the White House, but it don't mean a bean to those right wing politicos."

I opened my mouth to speak, but Alice grabbed my arm and steered me out of the kitchen towards the dining room.

"Enough of this political stuff - come and help me lay the table."

The meal was not long in coming: great chunks of cold turkey breast, cranberry sauce, sprouts and boiled potatoes, washed down with very rough and very cold French wine. I hadn't realised how hungry I was, and wolfed down my first plate of food before the girls had hardly begun.

Carol was impressed: "Gee, I haven't seen a guy eat that fast since our cheerleaders' party with the football team."

"Guys have hollow leg bones," Carly informed us, "I read it in *Playboy*. They need all that food to make their balls grow." She and Carol screeched with laughter in unison.

"God, d'you remember the size of the balls on those football players, Carol?" Carly continued. "They had us choose the guy with the biggest ones, and he then got to screw the girl with the biggest tits. But that was never us."

"It sounds absolutely barbarous," said Alice. "But then I've obviously led a sheltered life."

"Oh you English are such prudes" observed Carly.

The girls had some left-over pecan pie for dessert, and I devoured most of that for them with some relish. Then we all retired to the front room and collapsed into two large but rather battered sofas.

"Do you guys want some pot?" asked Carly after a few minutes.

Alice and I looked at one another. It was obvious that both of us were 'marijuana virgins'.

"Yes - great," we both answered, somewhat uncertainly.

"Right, there's nothing like a nice joint after a good meal," she said, and she went off to her secret store to procure the makings of what became four giant joints. Her rolling technique was a wonder to behold. My feeble efforts to make roll-ups from Gold Flake were always a disaster, with strands of tobacco splayed out at both ends. Carol, in the meantime had put on a Bob Dylan album, and as I began to inhale, the loud vibrant chords of *Mr Tambourine Man* pulsated in waves through my head, each note sharper and more beautiful than the preceding one. I couldn't decide whether it was the alcohol or the cannabis that was having the greater effect, though I didn't feel at all befuddled, as one usually does from alcohol, and everything seemed sharper, brighter and louder. After two or three more puffs, I abandoned any attempt at rational thought and just abandoned myself to the experience.

"Where d'you get this stuff – it's really good?" I asked.

Carly inhaled deeply, then blew three perfect smoke rings towards the ceiling.

"There's this real cool little club called the 'Green Carnation' just off the Bayswater Road" she said. "You can get pretty much anything there – hash, coke, acid – but we stick mostly to hash, less risky and cheaper too."

Carol poured us both some more wine. "The music's good too - you must come along some time." She pulled Carly out of her armchair.

"Now let's leave these two to get better acquainted while we go and have a rest" she said, winking at Carly. The American girls left the room and retired to the adjacent bedroom, and they were soon romping around like a couple of kids and giggling uncontrollably, or so it seemed to us from the noises coming through the wall. I glanced at Alice in a dreamy way.

"Sounds like fun, but not very restful," I commented, somewhat bemused.

"I think they prefer one another to boys," she suggested.

I would probably have been shocked had I not had a head full of pot. I hadn't met any lesbians before, though I had always assumed that girls did fool around with one another. Why not, they had so many interesting bits to explore. The mysterious places that always seemed to elude me.

"I hope you prefer boys."

As if in answer, she came over and sat on my lap. She took two swift drags to finish her joint, exhaled a huge lungful of aromatic smoke, then kissed me - as it says in the song - 'like I'd never been kissed before'. Her lovely lips, her small darting tongue, the warmth of her body through her soft lambswool jumper. I was in seventh heaven, floating on clouds of cannabis and desire. But suddenly I wasn't content with gorgeous kisses, and soon my hand was wandering up the inside of her jumper. The first touch of my fingertips on her skin caused her to freeze, but then she relaxed, and emboldened my hand rose to touch the outside of her lacy bra. Again she froze, then suddenly sat bolt upright and said "I want to go home now - I'm on another early turn tomorrow."

She climbed off my lap, looking down as she did so at the lump in my trousers.

"Besides, you don't look too comfortable."

My befuddled brain tried desperately to think of something original to say, but could only manage: "I'm a bit stiff - must be the way we were sitting."

She laughed as she pulled down her jumper and straightened her black corduroy skirt. "I thought you were going to say that your leg had gone to sleep - but I can see that it hasn't!"

There was a renewed burst of giggling from the confines of the bedroom and then a shriek and a gasp.

"Time to go, I think," said Alice. "Bye you two - thanks for dinner."

A moment's silence and then: "Bye you guys - come again some time, " from Carly.

"Yeah - you come right on back," from Carol.

"And thanks for the joints" I added. "We've had a really interesting time." I took Alice in my arms and hugged and kissed her passionately. I was in love!

I was feeling rather peculiar as we got into the car, either from the affects of the alcohol or the pot or the shock of the cold night air. Nowadays I would have left the car and taken the Tube, but things were much more casual in the sixties. I can't even remember whether we bothered to put on our seatbelts. We drove in silence down towards Euston, with me concentrating on the rather fuzzy traffic signals. It was about eleven and fortunately the roads were really quiet. We turned into the Marylebone Road and caught our first green light, and at 20 mph you can then catch them all, so we sailed all the way to Great Portland Street, hitting all the green lights. Then we took the rest of the lights at amber before turning into Gower Street, and it was then that the car behind put on his flashing blue light. I stopped the van outside UCL's main entrance and the police car stopped just behind. Two police officers got out and approached the van.

"Can you get out of the car sir?"

It is amazing how fast you can sober up when the need arises. I stepped out and stood ramrod stiff by the side of the van.

"Have you got your licence with you?"

I rooted around in my jacket and found my battered licence. A sheer fluke that it was there rather than somewhere else.

"What's the licence plate of the van?"

I gave him the details slowly and very precisely.

"D'you know what an amber signal means?"

"Get ready to stop," I suggested.

"So why didn't you?"

I thought very fast on my feet.

"My girlfriend's a nurse at UCH and she has to be in by 11.30 or she gets into trouble. I was in a hurry."

He peered into the car.

"All right – you're lucky this time – we like nurses. But don't do it in future."

"Thanks – I won't."

After a cursory glance at the tyres, which were, fortunately, relatively new, they wandered back to their patrol car. Thank God they didn't look at the exhaust pipe, which was held together with that resin stuff.

I drove on slowly to the nurses' home. Alice leant over and gave me a kiss on the cheek.

"That was pretty impressive – well done."

"Damn close all the same. Shame to spoil a great evening."

She gave me another kiss – this time on the lips.

"Yes I liked it too. You're the first boy I've allowed to get their hands up my jumper, though God knows how many over-sexed boys have tried."

Again my brain reeled to find something sensible to say, but all I could come up with was very trite.

"What can I say, I feel privileged" I said, though this was the second time in as many days that my efforts at breast fondling had been interrupted.

"It was nice though - too nice," she added, "and I'm scared about getting involved - but I do want to see you again."

"How about tomorrow?"

"Yes, I'm on a straight, so you could come round at about 5.30 again."

"Great - see you then," and with another peck on the cheek she was gone.

When I got home there was an overpowering smell of feet and a droning sound. A barefoot Hugh was lolling on our sofa, strumming his guitar and singing tunelessly.

"That girl friend of yours – Glenda or something - came round and left you a note - it's on the table." It was short and to the point.

Toby's been admitted to UCH with suspected rheumatic fever. Gaynor.

★ ★ ★ ★ ★

Gaynor and I arrived during afternoon visiting to find Toby in the middle of a blanket bath, hidden behind curtains. The half-suppressed squeaks and giggles suggested that Enid was assisting and that Toby was not a passive recipient of these ablutions. That his recovery was well under way was confirmed when the curtains around the bed were thrown open and the elfin-like Enid emerged. The damp patches on the front of her blouse revealed the object of Toby's attentions while she had been busy with the soap.

"As you can see, he's feeling better, back to his normal randy self," observed Enid.

"Has he been using absinthe again?" I suggested.

"No, penicillin and soluble aspirin - cheap and very effective. D'you know he's the first case of rheumatic fever they've seen here for 10 years."

"Yes, I'm quite a celebrity," Toby confirmed. "I've already been wheeled into a lecture theatre to have medical students feel the fluid in my swollen knees and put their cold stethoscopes on my heart to hear the murmur."

"How an earth did you catch this thing in the first place?" asked Gaynor.

"Too many nights in our cold, damp flat" suggested Enid, "the gas blew back one final time last week and we haven't had any heat since."

"But he's had that sore throat for weeks" I reminded her. "What's rheumatic fever anyway?"

I was suddenly aware of a presence behind me. "It starts with a haemolytic streptococcal infection" said a voice.

I turned to find a tallish man in a long white coat with a stethoscope suspended from his neck. He was probably not much older than us, but exuded that air of confidence and superiority that doctors have.

"Most of those infected get better quickly, but a few - like your friend here - react badly and start to produce antibodies that destroy the joints and may even damage one of the valves in the heart" he said. We all looked at Toby, suddenly worried about him.

"But your friend has been lucky. Thanks to penicillin and lots of soluble aspirin, he's going to make a speedy recovery."

"So I'd noticed" Enid agreed.

The doctor - a Registrar, according to his badge - moved to the bedside.

. "I'd like to examine you, if I may" he said, and he began to pull the curtains around the bed. We moved away and hung around, feeling awkward.

University College Hospital comprised a large redbrick, cruciform Victorian building with high ceilings, acres of white tiles and huge sash windows. Succeeding generations had tried to modernise it, but Florence Nightingale would still have felt perfectly at home. Alice claimed that the only concession to modernity was the use of automatic bedpan washers rather than manual washing. First-year nurses like Alice were not much better than skivvies, washing patients, emptying bedpans, serving meals, permanently subservient to doctors, and always in fear of the ward sister and especially the night sister. These imposing spinsters were the hospital matriarchs, and even received a grudging respect from the doctors, whose greater knowledge of medicine was often counterbalanced by a glaring lack of commonsense. It was true, then as now, that the doctors diagnosed the disease and the nurses made the patients better, but the former failed to acknowledge this and perpetuated the myth of their god-like status.

A typically arrogant young houseman now entered the ward and approached the bed. He was thin and weedy with a pencil moustache and the name badge revealed that he was Henry Rowbotham. He was, we learnt later, a distant relative of Enid.

" Hi. Is Toby behind those curtains?"

Gaynor nodded:

"Yes, and the Registrar is in there too."

"I'll just pop my head in."

He did so, and got roundly rebuked. "Get out!" bellowed the Registrar, and the medic ducked out like a scalded cat.

"Christ, it's not as if he's stark bollock naked or anything" he hissed between clenched teeth. "I am a sort of friend of the family after all. But who are you two anyway?"

"We work in the same lab as Toby" I told him, and his haughtiness suddenly turned to interest.

"Hey - do you know a bloke called Peter Sharpfoot? He works in Chemistry for a guy called Pewsey and I need to get hold of him."

"Yes - we know him. He's the obnoxious nerk who has just taken over our lab. You two should get on like a house on fire."

"You chemists are boring and smelly. Well if you see him, tell him I've got something for him." He sneered and turned on his heel and was gone.

Enid and the Registrar emerged from behind the curtains, and he pulled them around to reveal Toby sitting in bed buttoning up his pyjama jacket, a large grin on his face.

"You'll live. You have a slight heart murmur, but I think you've always had it, like ten per cent of the population. It's quite normal."

"How did he get rheumatic fever in the first place?" asked Enid, "Is it our damp cold flat?"

"Yes, possibly, but he most probably picked up the streptococci from someone on the Tube, and he is unlucky enough to have an immune system that reacted to it in a self-destructive way."

Like most patients Toby was interested in his drugs. "So the penicillin kills the bacteria, but what does the aspirin do?"

"Your joints are swollen and painful, so the aspirin's job is to reduce the inflammation and take away the pain and swelling. The ancient Egyptians did something similar with extracts of willow bark."

But the lesson was now clearly at an end. Inquisitive patients could only be tolerated for so long, and there were other patients to see.

"You'll probably need to stay in for a week or so, until the swelling has completely gone" said the Registrar. "I'll come and see you again tomorrow." He smiled weakly at Toby and Enid and then moved off to a bed at the end of the ward,

"Just as well we cleared out the lab yesterday before you decided to skive off," teased Gaynor,"

"Thanks for your concern," sneered Toby.

The tea trolley clattered onto the ward, manned by the usual (for that time) Spanish ward orderly.

"Tea or café? A nice bun for you meestair?"

Toby accepted the proffered tea and iced bun.

"For you meesas - you eez wife?"

Enid nodded and took her cup of tea, and the trolley moved off to the next bed.

"It was good to see that medical nerk get his come-uppance," I observed. "I can't recall his name."

"He's Henry Rowbotham, "replied Enid. "Your classic

public school medic. Thinks he knows everything and hands up your blouse while you're getting introduced. He's my second cousin, works on the gynae ward. Wonder why he's so keen to see that guy Peter Sharpfoot?"

"Two of a kind - nerks of the world unite," suggested Gaynor,

Toby seemed tired, so Gaynor and I left the ward and returned to the lab. There were still a few odds and ends to be removed, and we gave the teak benches a quick clean and polish just so no one could accuse us of leaving the lab in a state. The acid burns and the partially-combusted end of one of the benches, were a reminder of past accidents that had been amusing rather than dangerous.

As we were carrying the last few items across the corridor into the large lab opposite - our new home - Peter Sharpfoot appeared, his face adorned with a leer from ear to ear.

"Glad to see you're almost done - we need to get on with our new work" he grinned.

"Oh piss off, " retorted Gaynor, "you make my flesh creep." Not to be outdone, he came back at her with: "And talking about creeps - have you heard the latest about your boss?"

"I'm sure we're not interested" I told him.

But Gaynor clearly was. "OK creep - what's the latest?"

"You won't believe the old boy had it in him, or had it in her, more like" he said, guffawing at his own feeble joke, "He's been interfering with one of his third year tutees in the privacy of his office. Dirty old sod."

"Oh sod off," snorted Gaynor and pushed past him down the corridor.

"Don't believe me then? Well it'll be all over the College tomorrow - you'll see."

Neither of us believed him, but he was right on all counts. The whole place was soon buzzing with rumour and innuendo. Needless to say there were several versions of the story, but the gist of it was that our Prof had been alone in his office with Sophia, one of the more voluptuous third-year students, ostensibly helping her with her tutorial problems, but he had ended up squeezing her breasts. They were certainly a temptation that most of us had considered in idle moments, but the thought of RAJ giving them a squeeze was preposterous. The girl made a formal complaint and RAJ got a call from the Dean and then the Provost. All of this was supposed to have been hushed up, but Pewsey seemed determined to disseminate the rumours and worse. Each new story was more fanciful than its predecessor. At their most extreme they had the girl stripped off on the carpet with RAJ banging away like a young stud. Unbelievable stuff, but it caused a major stir in the College.

I duly met Alice from her straight shift at 5.30. We headed for the Bonfini, a quiet little Italian coffee bar near Warren Street Station. Over a cup of frothy coffee and a shared plate of pasta, she revealed that her day had also been marred by unwanted sexual advances.

"This creep of a houseman got me cornered in the sluice and started chatting me up. Hands everywhere as well."

"Sounds like the public school nerd we saw on the ward - Rowbotham or something."

"Yes - that's him."

"He's Enid's second cousin - she has a pretty poor opinion of him too."

"I can't fathom why these medics all think they are God's gifts to women - they're mainly jerks who don't know one end of a woman from the other. You should see them in the delivery room. The midwives usually send them away and only call them back for the stitching. They usually make a pig's ear of that too."

She was silent for a minute and then added: "I also surprised him at the drugs cupboard. I thought he was filching some Panadol for a headache, but he'd actually got some ampoules of ergometrine."

"What's that for?"

"We give it to mothers who bleed a lot after the birth - it contracts the blood vessels in the uterus. Not the sort of thing anyone would want."

"It all sounds incredibly messy to me, the things you girls have to put up with - the curse, having babies..."

"Blokes groping you all the time," she interjected.

"I hope you're not including me in that category."

"No - I like your brand of gentle groping - that was nice the other night."

And then as if she had suddenly remembered: "D'you fancy a trip to the seaside this weekend? I want to go home to see my parents and I was hoping to persuade you to come too.

I'm sure Mum and Dad would love to see my new boyfriend." She pronounced 'boyfriend' with inverted commas. Well, it was very early days.

"OK - sounds great - I'll clean the van.."

* * * * *

Henri-Louis Pernod stood alongside the large copper retort which held 1000 litres of undistilled liquor. He could feel the heat radiating from the vessel as the coal-fired boiler fed energy to its base. Soon the colourless liquid would begin dripping from the attached condenser into the large glass collecting vessel. A complex aroma incorporating the volatile constituents of hyssop, fennel, and wormwood, mingled with the intoxicating vapours of 120 proof alcohol, emanated from the bottling room next door. Ten local women were pushing home the corks into full bottles and applying the distinctive Pernod Fils labels which bore a white cross on a red background and the word *absinthe*. His product was now popular all over Europe and as far away as San Francisco and New Orleans. On the boulevards of Paris they now referred to *l'heure d'absinthe*, when everyone stopped for the evening aperitif. He had seen reproductions of artworks by Degas, Van Gogh and Toulouse Lautrec, all depicting the use of absinthe, and felt that what he now called his 'invention' had really made an impact.

He felt a warm glow of achievement. This new factory on the banks of the River Doubs in Pontarlier deep within the Jura was now producing 1400 litres of absinthe each day. The bank manager had been only too pleased to lend him the money for the large tract of land and the building costs of the factory - not least because he had experienced the benefits of absinthe himself. There had been some initial opposition from the local priest – several vigorous sermons warning of the dangers of unbridled passion brought on by this evil new drink - but most of the men of Pontarlier had opted for the immediate benefits of absinthe rather than the uncertainties of their entrance into Paradise. Their wives, girlfriends and (in many cases) the partners of their illicit couplings were also favourably disposed to the enhanced performance of their lovers. Even the priest could not pretend he disapproved of the number of growing bellies that presaged an enlargement of his flock. It was, however, a problem for Henri-Louis, since several of his bottling girls had become pregnant just as he had got them fully trained in their jobs.

At the thought of these new children, Henri-Louis experienced a sudden twinge of remorse. His recent success had been won at a price and he now regretted the long hours that had kept him away from home and his family. He would never forget the look of anguish on his young wife's face as she held their darling daughter – their first child, aged only three – when he had returned home after two days' absence at the distillery. When he had left she had been recovering from measles – still scarlet in the face but immeasurably better than a few days previously. Only the large spot on her left eye spoiled the beauty of her angelic face. She had scratched the spot and made it bleed, and now her left eyelid was puffy and partly closed. But she seemed to be on the mend and he knew nothing of the septicaemia that would carry her off with such rapidity. His wife, frantic with fear and desperation, had tried to recall him from the factory, but he had brushed aside her concerns and told her not to worry. The village doctor had prescribed a poultice made from willow bark, and this had eased the inflammation, but a savage bacterial infection, untreatable in those pre-antibiotic days, had ravaged her young body and carried her off within 48 hours. His wife was inconsolable, and Henri knew that she blamed him for their loss and that their relationship would never be the same.

He emerged from his reverie to see the local notary, Eustace de Séverin, distracting one of the prettier women, Florence La Fosse, from her labours in the bottling section. Their conversation appeared animated and intimate, as if between two teenage lovers, and he noted that de Severin was stroking her bare arm tenderly. Yet Henri-Louis knew that Florence was the mother of two young children and had no business flirting with this suave young man. The notary looked up and saw Pernod standing on the threshold of the bottling room. He waved and, touching Florence affectionately on the arm, moved towards him, hand outstretched to shake his hand.

"*Bonjour M. Pernod, vous allez bien?*"

"*Oui - vous aussi?*"

"*Oui, bien sûr* - it's always a pleasure to come here and visit one of my most successful clients, especially when I suspect that you have some more business for me."

Pernod disliked de Séverin: he was envious of his good

looks and easy way with women. He guessed that he had formed liaisons with several girls in the village and didn't want him interfering with his bottling women. But it was his cockiness that grated the most. However, he was a very good negotiator when it came to prising money from the bankers. Pernod motioned towards a small office at the side of the bottling room.

"Come - let's discuss my new plans."

The plan was simple - the distillery was already too small to meet the growing demand for absinthe, and the present site was too cramped to accommodate any further expansion. However, on the other side of the river, close to the town cemetery, there was a huge plot of land with a fast-flowing stream running through it. This would make an ideal site for a new, bigger distillery. The problems, however, seemed insuperable, since the land belonged to the church.

"So that is my desire and also my problem - what do you suggest?"

Eustace appeared to ponder the problem for some moments, but in reality he had already conceived a plan.

"I think I may have a solution - but it will be expensive. How much is the site worth to you?"

Pernod considered his position.

"I could probably stretch to 3000 gold napoleons - but only for a clear-cut solution."

"And my fee would be ten percent of the purchase price."

There was a sharp intake of breath from Pernod.

"*Mon Dieu* – that's extortion."

"Precisely – that's exactly what I intend to carry out on that priest! He won't know what's hit him."

Pernod hesitated for a moment, then he nodded. The fee was truly extortionate, but the prize was huge.

"*D'accord* – see you in a week."

De Séverin left with a flourish, brushing Madame La Fosse's bare arm with his hand as he left the bottling room . Pernod was sure that he heard him whisper "*à bientôt,*" as he passed her.

★ ★ ★ ★ ★

Alice's mother poured a thick, coal-black gravy onto the thin slices of over-cooked roast beef on my plate. Roast potatoes, boiled potatoes, a flattened Yorkshire pudding and four other vegetables jostled for position in the viscous liquid, though space was rather limited. She turned her attention to her husband's plate, which had even less free space. He had been summoned from his labours in the garage, which Alice had described as his 'Wombling space'. It was here that he fashioned all manner of strange creations using almost any conceivable cast-off household object. Several of these creations were dotted around the dining room. They included a number of Christmas decorations that had missed the Twelfth Night clearance, and the most striking of these were cardboard cutouts of what appeared to be overly well-endowed angels blowing trumpets. The mantelpiece sported what appeared to be a metallic tree displaying jewellery, but on closer examination turned out to be pieces of Meccano bolted together and bearing pieces of coloured glass which twinkled in the firelight. I also noted that two of the wine glasses on the table had broken stems which had been glued back together with great globs of polystyrene cement.

Mrs Bolton, a small jolly woman with jet black hair - she had evidently dyed it very recently, because some of the dye had adhered to her neck and ears - continued her circumnavigation with the gravy jug. She hesitated, jug poised over Alice's plate, which was largely devoid of food.

"Alice dear, you've hardly enough to keep a budgie alive."

"I'm fine Mum. For goodness sake sit down and have your dinner."

"She does look awfully thin," observed Mr Bolton. "Don't they feed you in that hospital?"

"Don't fuss Dad, I'm always snacking in the ward pantry."

Alice's father was certainly the very opposite of thin, a tribute to the huge meals that Mrs B served him and his predilection for stout and mild at his local on a Friday evening. On the way down to Bournemouth Alice had told me of the Friday routine.

"My Mum would have my brother and me in bed with her before he rolled home from the pub, just to make sure he took himself off to the boxroom. It was all a bit of a joke - she didn't like the smell of beer and fags but she never objected to his Friday drinking because she knew he had a boring job as a stock control clerk, and he always handed over most of his pay packet before he headed for the pub."

The food was great, though it was clear that every last drop of fat from the meat had been recycled into the gravy, and the strawberry crumble, when it arrived, took its flavour from the butter dish rather than the tin of strawberries. Mr B's girth was certainly unsurprising. He now watched the jug of custard like a hawk as it passed around the table, fearing no doubt that it would be exhausted before it reached his ample portion of crumble - but it arrived safely.

"Why don't you show Philip our beach hut?" suggested Mrs B, "I've just put up some new curtains."

"Oh Mum - why would he want to do that."

"No really - it sounds like a great idea - take in some sea air," I agreed with Mrs B.

"Then you could come back for some tea."

Alice was still reluctant to go.

"What about the washing up, Mum? We can't just leave you all the mess."

"That's all right, your father will do it, won't you George." George grunted through a mouthful of crumble and custard. "Besides - he'll only doze off if I don't keep him busy – just like he used to when he was on guard duty." Mr Bolton harrumphed.

It seemed that Mr Bolton had had a good war in the sense that he never saw a German, and had travelled as far afield as Norway, Iceland and India with the Royal Artillery. The long tedious hours manning gun emplacements with nothing to fire at had induced frequent bouts of lethargy, and every time he reached the elevated rank of Lance Bombardier, he was demoted back to the rank of Gunner for being found asleep at his post. This was an oft-repeated family joke. I guess he was lucky - in the First World War he would probably have been shot.

So we ended up in the beach hut with its new pink gingham curtains, its Calor gas cooker, and pile of abandoned deckchairs. It had that musty, locked-up-for-the-winter smell, combined with a faint whiff of cheap suntan oil and seaweed. A light sprinkling of sand adhered to the edges where the last dustpan and brush of summer had failed to lift it.

"Well - here's the famous beach hut - what now - a cup of tea I guess."

Alice's mother had insisted we take two teabags, a few sachets of sugar, a medicine bottle of milk, and a thermos of water.

"You're sure to want a cup of tea while you're down there," she had insisted. She was totally right, but for the wrong reason. We needed a mug of tea just to warm our hands after the freezing walk down the chine and along the windswept seafront, with a bitter east wind sweeping up the Solent. An English seafront in winter under a grey leaden sky, with flurries of sand swirling off the beach, is a grim cold place. We closed the door and pulled the curtains. Alice opened up the valve of the Calor gas tank and lit one of the two burners on the stove. The contents of the thermos went into a flimsy aluminium kettle with one of those whistling caps on its spout, and suddenly the place seemed a whole lot cosier.

I glanced across at Alice; she was shivering as she reached

into the wall-mounted cupboard for two mugs. Her knitted woollen bonnet framed her small features, and her tight black winter coat made her appear smaller than she was - waif-like in fact. I had an urge to envelop her and keep her warm.

"You cold?" I asked rhetorically.

"Bloody frozen - my mother wants shooting."

"Come and have a hug."

I pulled her towards me, wrapping my arms around her.

"Sorry you've had to suffer this. It's so much nicer in the summer, sitting on the sea wall in the sunshine and watching all the little kids playing on the beach."

"Is this where you brought all your boyfriends?" I was probing her past love-life.

She laughed. "You have to be joking – if any of the boys I went out with had got in here, I'd have needed brute force to fight them off. The summer French boys were the worst – so much more experienced that the English boys. We never got further than the sand dunes at Sandbanks and even there they were after a lot more than French kissing. It's damn hard staying a virgin."

"And is that the way you intend to stay?"

She looked coyly at me.

"Well – I have these good intentions, but it is getting harder to keep up my defences."

And all in a rush we were kissing. My hands were inside her coat, underneath her grey lambswool jumper, reaching for her breasts, finding them. She gasped, and I held her tightly to me.

Then there was a loud knocking on the glass of the door.

"Anyone there? - police -open up!"

The door burst open and a large, florid face under a police helmet peered into the hut.

"What's going on in there?"

My hands were suddenly at my side and Alice was explaining that her mother owned the hut and that we were down from London.

"We've had lots of break-ins recently," he explained. "Right you two, get along home, when you've had your tea. Be sure to lock up well."

And he was gone as quickly as he had arrived. We looked at one another and began to laugh.

"Phew - my honour saved by a ploddy," laughed Alice.

"He's gone now. There's still time to remedy that."

"No there isn't - your hands are too bloody cold anyway."

The kettle began to sing and the water bubbled out of the spout.

"You can jolly well drink this tea though. Mother will certainly ask us if we enjoyed it."

And she did. We stayed for another cup of tea and a piece of Battenberg cake, and then headed back to London - a slow drive in the battered van. Alice was very quiet on the way back, despite my attempts to get her talking about her parents and her job. Eventually she confided that she was worried about work. Ward Sister had called a meeting for the next morning – after the patients had had their breakfast and washes but before the Consultants' ward rounds began. One of the other nurses had heard rumours that the meeting was to be about discrepancies in the drug cupboard inventory, and Alice was worried that she should say something about Henry Rowbotham and his apparent theft of ergometrine. I told her that she should – he sounded like a real creep and deserved to get his come-uppance.

I dropped Alice off at the nurses' home, having made arrangements to see her later in the week, then stopped off to see Toby and Enid on the way home. Toby was now well on the road to recovery, and Enid had left him at home looking after Jonathan while she resumed her studies. We were drinking coffee when the lovely old Mauritian caretaker knocked on the door. He was in a state of agitation and wheezy from the climb up the stairs, and handed a scribbled note to Toby.

"A friend called – he eez in trouble with zer poliss – he needs *une personne pour un référence.*"

It seemed that Deepak had been arrested and taken to Tottenham Court Road police station and needed one of us to vouch for him. Toby clearly couldn't go, so I assumed the role of Good Samaritan.

★ ★ ★ ★ ★

Deepak's day had begun well. As usual he had skipped his lectures at LSE to attend to his business interests. He made a morning visit to his contact in East London to purchase a gross of contraceptives, then a lunchtime session in the Union bar at LSE to supply the needs of his regular student clients.

He even found some new customers – eager young first years desperate to lose their virginity as soon as they could ensnare a girl at one of the Union hops. Deepak knew they had little chance of success, since first-year girls usually fell prey to second-year wolves - all of whom he already supplied with condoms.

His evening was mapped out: an early evening rendezvous with a new girl he had 'pulled' the previous week. A few drinks in the Union bar, then back to his flat in Westbourne Park Road for an evening of seduction. At four his plans began to unravel when he checked his mail and found a note from this new girl, standing him up. He was in her tutorial group at LSE where both were studying Business Management. She thought he was charming and good-looking and the stories about his father's airline were fascinating, but his constant references to her great body, though flattering, were suspicious. The warning from a friend, who had learned at first hand of Deepak's enthusiasm for seduction, convinced her that an invitation to dinner at his place would inevitably lead to a fight to keep him from trying to get her into bed. His reputation for first-date seductions was too great to risk – she was interested in a more lasting relationship.

With an empty evening yawning before him, Deepak remembered the invitation from James, the gay musician who lived downstairs from him, to visit the Green Carnation, a small club off the Bayswater Road, to hear his jazz quintet perform in their debut gig. Despite his mistrust of anyone who did not share his own overactive preference for the opposite sex, there was an empty evening to be filled, so Deepak made his way along Westbourne Park Road, now dark, cold and drab on this February evening, and found the club just round the corner from Whiteleys, off Queensway.

James' quintet was already in full swing and Deepak had to admit that the sound was pretty good. He perched on a stool by the bar and ordered a vodka and lime. James waved to acknowledge he had seen Deepak arrive. Deepak couldn't see much through the fug of smoke and dim lighting, and a sense of unease pervaded him when he perceived an unnecessary touching of hands as the barman handed over the drink, but this was nothing compared to the pressure he suddenly felt on his bottom which overhung the stool. He leapt to his feet, only just saving his drink from toppling.

"Bloody hell! Get your hands off! " he exclaimed as he turned to find a pretty boy leering at him.

"Oooh I am so sorry - did you spill your drink?"

"No thanks to you if I had!"

"Are you here by yourself - or are you with someone?"

Deepak felt threatened and disgusted.

"Look mate, I'm only interested in girls and don't want anything you're offering - so bugger off!"

"Well - suit yourself then - I'm sure I don't mind," and he minced off away from the bar.

The quintet reached the end of their first session and James came and joined Deepak at the bar.

"Nice music, shame about the audience in here" observed Deepak.

"Quite a mixed bunch, I must admit - some really nice guys though."

"Yeah – a bit too nice for me."

"Where's your girl tonight, Deepak?"

"Cow stood me up."

"God - and you the most desirable bloke in London! How about something to take your mind off your problems?"

"Not if it's like the last stuff you sold me - it didn't do a thing for me."

James rummaged around in his jacket and pulled out an envelope, and then from this a small circle of paper.

"What the hell's that? It looks like the filter paper we used to have at school."

"This stuff will blow you away. It's acid, LSD. Remember we were discussing it at Toby and Enid's dinner party."

"I've read about it in *Rolling Stone* magazine - all those cool dudes in California use it and get really freaky. Timothy Leary telling people to 'turn on and tune in'."

"That's it – two hundred and fifty quid a paper."

"Jesus that's a rip off!"

"Yes, but you cut it up into smaller pieces. You can use some and then flog the rest. Come on - a rich kid like you can afford some."

Deepak thought about it for a moment. It was very expensive, but the temptation to try something new - and illegal - was too great.

"OK, I'll take it - but it better be good." He counted out the notes and took possession of the envelope. "This stuff better work."

"It will, believe me, it's gonna blow your mind."

James was summoned back to the quintet for the second half, and Deepak left the club to šeek female company before he was molested again. He found the nearest callbox and phoned several of his girlfriends. Most were out, but he eventually managed to persuade a Spanish girl called Juanita, who was also having a dull evening, to meet him at his flat for supper and some drinks. As he left the callbox he failed to notice the dark car that pulled away from the kerb and began following him along the road.

Back at the flat, he had a quick bath, changed into some loose trousers and a T-shirt, put a Beatles LP on the Dansette, and poured himself a gin and tonic. The bell rang as he took his first mouthful of the G and T, and he had to admit to himself, as he let Juanita in, that she was rather nice. She took off her winter coat but retained her feather boa. Deepak loved her flashing brown eyes and gorgeous full breasts, and most important of all, she actually seemed genuinely pleased to see him, and gave him a long, open-mouthed kiss immediately. She emptied the contents of a small bag, revealing a bag of rice, a tin of salmon and a small French stick.

"I will feex us some risotto - you like?"

"Great - I'll open a bottle of wine - red or white."

"Red - *por favor*," and she disappeared into the kitchen to begin cooking.

Deepak was unsure when to sample the acid. If he had too much to drink he wouldn't be able to tell whether it was the drink or the acid that was causing the trip. Alternatively, it might be risky to take the stuff on an empty stomach. He decided to compromise. There was a small bag of salted peanuts on the coffee table, so he ate these, then consumed a small piece of the filter paper and lolled on the sofa waiting for something to happen. Juanita was singing quietly in the kitchen and he could hear the clatter of utensils and pans. The Beatles continued in their melodic way and the central heating clanked away in the background. Nothing seemed to be happening and he quietly cursed James for selling him such an expensive load of rubbish, but then the light bulb suddenly became the most vivid rainbow he had ever seen, the Beatles' lyrics became sharper and the notes so crisp he could almost feel them. His arms and legs were floating away as if they were a raft on the sea. He tried to get off the sofa but could not, and his voice, when he called out to Juanita, appeared to rise from his throat as a high-pitched squeak. This turned into a scream of fear as a raven-haired Aztec priestess appeared at his side, wearing a feathered costume, and brandishing an obsidian knife. With a superhuman effort, he rose from the sofa and grappled the knife from her grasp, tearing at her costume until she was naked on the floor beneath him. She, for her part, seemed to welcome this savagery, and tore at his clothes in reciprocation. Deepak soon found himself engaged in a wild and frenzied sexual coupling which reached a climax like no other he had experienced, the blood rushing through his body with a sound like Niagara Falls. Juanita loved it too and was merely curious as to why he had torn the French stick from her hands as he grappled her to the floor.

* * * * *

Henry Rowbotham came upon the entrance to the farm unexpectedly, and had to swerve to miss the metal gatepost as he turned into the narrow driveway. The red MG Midget his father had given him for his 21st birthday already had several bumps and scrapes from past encounters with hard objects. The directions to the farm had been extremely vague and Henry was both relieved and pleased with himself now that he had found this backwater outside Hambledon near Henley on Thames. A dog began barking as soon as it heard the scrunch of his tyres on the gravel. A gangly young man in a holey jumper peered from the barn to the right of the main farm building..

"Hello Henry, hope you've not been followed?"

"No - sure - I haven't seen a living thing since Henley."

"Right - move the car into those trees, then come on in and I'll show you the set-up. Have you got some more stuff?"

Henry pulled a packet from his pocket. "I've managed to get a few ampoules. I hope it's enough to keep you going for a while, cos the staff on the ward are getting really nosey."

He parked the car and joined Peter Sharpfoot inside the barn. The air was laden with an acrid smell, and he started to cough immediately.

"Christ what's that? How d'you work in this atmosphere?"

"Just thionyl chloride. A bit of SO_2 and HCl will tone up your lungs a treat - clear out all those nasty smoggy deposits you've picked up in London.'

Henry Rowbotham had first met Peter Sharpfoot at Harrow, not because they were in the same class but because they shared the weekly cleaning of a bren gun as members of the Harrow cadet force. In those post-war years and with national service still a looming menace, most boys at public schools and even some grammar schools, were coerced into membership of the school cadet forces. The mindless weekly tasks of applying blanco to gaiters and belts and molten polish to the toecaps of big black boots was nothing compared to the discomfort of having to wear khaki trousers that chafed and itched like mad. This and the incessant marching, wheeling and turning to orders barked by older boys who had been awarded three stripes, more often than not for 'arse-licking', was a cross that had to be borne, along with the cold showers and the undercurrent of homosexuality. The only 'perk' that rendered membership of the cadet force bearable was the opportunity to handle big, complicated weapons while cleaning them. All members of the cadet force had their own Lee Enfield .303 rifle, while two shared a bren gun and half a dozen shared the task of cleaning the school's only 25-pounder. For legal and safety reasons, the firing pins were missing from all of these weapons, though that did not stifle the subversive and imaginative plans dreamt up during cleaning sessions. One nice big 25-pound shell would cream the prefects' room, while a long burst from a bren would mow down the emerging survivors. Such was the stuff of dreams.

After their A Levels, Henry had started the long haul of a medical degree at UCH, while Peter had gone to Exeter

University to study Chemistry. Their paths had recrossed when Peter arrived to work as a postdoc with Pewsey at Empire University, and their common need for money had driven them to explore illicit ventures. For a while, like Deepak, they dealt in black market condoms, selling these to their fellow students at knock-down prices, but the profit margin was very small and it also brought them into contact with various shady and rather nasty black marketeers. The chance of a physical confrontation had suddenly become quite likely, and the wielding of a flick knife at one of their recent meetings had convinced them that it was time to move on to other enterprises.

Henry came from a sub-aristocratic family who had lived in Shropshire for generations. There was a long association with the medical profession, and one of his ancestors had even worked for a time alongside Erasmus Darwin, though his subsequent membership of the Lunar Society was a prelude to more doubtful activities. Henry's father had drunk his way through most of the family fortune following a disastrous investment in a Darwin memorabilia shop in Shrewsbury. The replicas of the Beagle and Galapagos finches were some 50 years ahead of their time, as in post-war Britain people preferred to spend their limited resources on the meagre rations of meat and clothing.

Peter Sharpfoot, whose father was a Professor of Chemistry at the University of Portsmouth, could at least claim to have an academic background. Unfortunately, his father was mostly known for his eccentric views on homosexuality, which he believed was due to a deficiency of zinc in the diet. His public lectures on the subject were inevitably accompanied by much heckling and many ribald comments, and his written expostulations were poorly received. The one thing Peter and Henry had in common was a serious lack of money, hence their need for money-making schemes.

Recently there had been a chance encounter with James in the Green Carnation, and several interesting hallucinatory experiences persuaded them of the profits to be had from the illicit manufacture of LSD. Their access to the necessary chemicals and the drug ergometrine were an opportunity not to be missed.

"So who owns this farm?" enquired Henry. "And does he know what you're up to?"

"That's my secret - but he was the one who showed me how to do the chemistry on the lab scale."

Peter stopped talking while he fetched a drum marked with a skull and cross bones and labelled diethylamine. "Go over to that chest freezer and fetch me the bag of ice you'll find inside" he said.

Henry complied, dragging the large bag over to a glass apparatus clamped to a tall metal stand. Peter lowered the large, three-necked round glass flask into a huge plastic bowl.

"OK - now pour all of the ice into this bowl while I get the amine into the dropping funnel."

Henry tipped the ice in, then watched as Peter poured some of the diethylamine into the pear-shaped vessel that sat in one of the side-openings of the flask.

"OK, stand back - this can get quite exciting," he said, and he opened the large tap at the base of the funnel and carefully controlled the rate of addition of the amine to the contents of the large flask, now well cooled by the ice. There was a loud hiss and a cloud of white smoke as the first drops hit the surface of the liquid, which was being stirred vigorously by a paddle stirrer that entered the flask by its central opening. The liquid became steadily darker, but the hissing lessened in intensity and there was less vapour produced as the addition proceeded.

"Right - time for a couple of pints at the pub before work-up and purification."

"Really - is it safe to leave?"

"Sure," Peter reassured him, " I've had no problems so far, and we can also use the stuff you've brought to start off another batch when we get back."

They took Henry's car to a pub in Hambledon, a quaint hunters' inn at the end of the village track and on the edge of open fields bordered by a thick wooded hillside. The bar was dark and smoky, but the light was good enough to make eye contact with two village girls, one plump and the other skinny, who flirted with them from the start, and it was soon evident that three or four vodka and limes and several bags of salt and vinegar crisps might be enough to secure an evening of passion. The first part of the plan worked well, and there was certainly no problem persuading them to come back to the farm, though squeezing them both into the jump seat of the Midget proved to be difficult. In the end, Peter and the skinny one managed to fold themselves into the back seat, and Henry drove off with the plump one singing at the top of her surprisingly tuneful voice. It was a mere three miles back to the farm, but the sound of singing grew louder all the way, punctuated by squeaks from the jump seat as Peter used the enforced proximity of bodies to explore various parts of his girl's anatomy. Finally after much erratic driving, Henry swerved into the farm driveway and screeched to a halt - just inches from a police car that was parked at the front of the barn. One of the officers came over to Henry's side of the car.

"Excuse me sir, but there's been complaints from the next farm about foul smells" he said.

★ ★ ★ ★ ★

The police officers found Deepak *in flagrante* with Juanita, after they had forced the door of his flat at around ten in the morning. The police had, of course, seen it all before and showed only a passing interest in Juanita as she covered herself in a sheet and looked bemused. Deepak was much more concerned and became increasingly agitated as the police emptied the contents of his drawers and cupboards onto the bedroom floor. It took a mere five minutes for them to find what they were looking for – the remains of the Whatman filter paper. They did not examine the paper, since their instructions had been most explicit on that point - just to find the paper and bring it back for forensic examination. The substance with which it was impregnated was none of their business. They were just there to collect the evidence..

"It's a filter paper - I'm a chemist, we use them for routine filtration," Deepak lied trying to sound casual and surprised at their interest in something so benign, but also deeply hurt by the mess and commotion. "And how dare you mess up my flat."

"You'd better come with us - and you miss - get dressed and go home before you get involved."

Juanita needed no second bidding and was out of the bed and into her discarded knickers and bra before the policemen could even catch sight of her shapely body, though they both tried.

Deepak was hauled off to Tottenham Court Road police station, and that was where I met Gaynor, whose help and support I had elicited – I thought that two character references would be better than one. At first the police would not allow us to see him and we spent an hour in a draughty room with a weird assortment of London's least attractive residents, most of whom could have stepped from the pages of a Dickens novel. One old woman, who from the smell of her had been relieved of a gin bottle on arrival, spent the whole time caterwauling about "'er Jim", who was being beaten up by the rozzers "just 'cos he was caught pissing up against the door of the Westminster Bank". A middle-aged man with a forest of side-whiskers but little hair on top, and sporting a large red-spotted handkerchief in the breast pocket of his suit with tie to match, confided that his snappy suit and accessories had been purchased that very morning from his tailor in Savile Row. The police had made the outrageous suggestion that they had been taken from the changing room at Hepworths, a suggestion that would be libellous if it wasn't so risible given the humble nature of those premises and the fact that their suits were fit only for the general populace. And finally, a girl in her late teens with two black eyes and a baby on and off the breast, albeit under her jumper, who claimed that her Lenny "hadn't meant to 'it me - it were just an accident".

Finally we were allowed to see Deepak, who was clearly very scared and whose dishevelled appearance supported his contention that his interrogators had been rather rough.

"God - they're a bunch of bullying bastards. I've contacted my Old Man and he'll get them - I'm a citizen of Hong Kong for Chrissake."

"Deepak, what have you been up to?" Gaynor asked him

"Nothing!"

"Oh come on, you've been selling pot again."

"No, of course not!"

But he had admitted, under pressure, to buying the filter paper from a man in a pub who told him it was soaked in 'acid', though he hadn't given James away.

"How much did you pay for the stuff?"

"£250."

"Bloody hell - that's a fortune for us - I hope the trip was worth it."

Deepak rolled his eyes, recalling the time he had spent with Juanita.

"Can you ask the bastards to let me out of here - I'm innocent!"

We did so, but the police did not let him out for a further 48 hours, until the family lawyer kicked up a fuss and got him bail. By then everything was all over.

As we were leaving the police station, another 'old friend' was just arriving, ashen-faced and firmly handcuffed to a burly constable. It was Enid's obnoxious cousin Henry Rowbotham. He glanced at us in half-recognition but he could not quite recall where he had seen us.

"Couldn't happen to a nicer guy," observed Gaynor, "I wonder what the little creep has done."

"I'm sure Alice told me she had caught him with his fingers in the drugs cabinet." I was desperately trying to remember what he had been stealing. That mystery was unravelled later in the day - but with tragic consequences.

★ ★ ★ ★ ★

We never discovered the exact sequence of events, but it appears that RAJ asked Pewsey to come to his office - ostensibly to break the news that he was going to resign. We do know what they said to one another, because RAJ left a tape recorder running throughout the meeting. The recording begins with RAJ's invitation to come in.

"I hope you're serious about this resignation," Pewsey is heard to declare.

"Of course - how can I remain when they're determined to hound me over this alleged dalliance with the girl."

"You're a dirty old man and deserve to get the boot."

There is the sound of glasses and a cork being withdrawn.

"A toast then to my retirement and your success in ousting me from my research labs. Will you have glass of absinthe?"

"Is that the filthy muck that you make in the lab?"

"No, this is the genuine article, you can still buy it in parts of Spain - if you know where to look."

There is a short pause before Pewsey exclaims:

"God - that's bitter!"

"It's certainly an acquired taste. Here, try a little sugar with it."

Another pause.

"Tell me Pewsey - and I promise I won't tell a soul - where are you getting the ergometrine?"

"What!" A snort of indignation or surprise "What are you suggesting?"

"Come now, I'm not stupid or blind. Your postdoc Peter Sharpfoot is using my old lab to make LSD. He's even left the empty ampoules of ergometrine in the rubbish bin - not a very bright lad I am afraid."

"Er - he's using it as the starting material in his synthesis of that malodorous alkaloid pongoene," replies Pewsey after some hesitation.

"Hmmm - not very credible, especially with the bottle of diethylamine around."

"OK - but you can't prove it - and anyway you'll be gone soon."

"True, but so will you. How are your legs?"

There is silence, then the sound of someone slumping into a chair.

"What d'you mean – hey, what have you put in this drink?"

"You've obviously never read Plato. How does it go… *'and the man who gave the poison began to examine his feet and legs… and asked if there was any feeling in it, and Socrates said No… and so higher and higher and showed us that he was cold and stiff'*. That's the bit in the *Phaedo* where they poison Socrates with hemlock."

"God! You bastard! Help me - I can't breathe."

There is the sound of a chair falling over and a phone falling off the desk onto the floor and some scrabbling around and babbling, but nothing coherent - and then silence before the loud click of the tape recorder.

The College authorities broke into the office later that evening and found the two bodies. A post-mortem revealed that Pewsey had indeed died from hemlock poisoning and RAJ had taken an overdose of scopolamine - a more pleasant way to die. A trawl through RAJ's papers revealed some letters from UCH and appointment cards, and further investigations revealed that he had been recently diagnosed with inoperable bowel cancer. He had chosen a less painful exit strategy.

And that was about the end of the story. The authorities hushed up the LSD manufacture, though Henry Rowbottom and Peter Sharpfoot got 10 years apiece. The student who had accused RAJ of moral turpitude withdrew her accusations when she heard of his death - it was subsequently discovered that she had accused her chemistry teacher at school of similar sexual interference, in a futile attempt to get her mock A Level marks improved.

It would be nice to say that my relationship with Alice blossomed, but she sent me a 'dear John' note the very next day. Something about her really liking me but not being ready for a serious relationship. I was really gutted. Somehow Gaynor, Toby and I all cobbled together enough research results to write our theses about thujone, and although we missed out on advice from RAJ, we managed to survive our vivas and receive our PhDs. With great reluctance we left the uncomplicated and almost surreal confines of university to work for a living in the real world; but none of us ever forgot those few weeks at the beginning of 1965 when, as in a previous age, absinthe was so inextricably involved with sex and violent death.

★ ★ ★ ★ ★

Florence La Fosse lost her virginity at fifteen and had her first child at sixteen. She had found Jean La Fosse's muscular physique and his tales of far-off countries so alluring, and his forceful seduction was way beyond her ability to resist. Her parents were only too pleased to be rid of her, once her belly revealed the extent of her involvement with the ex-legionnaire.

At first her enjoyment of the new baby and the satisfaction of being married to a handsome, muscular man kept her contented. But that was before she discovered his love of drink, especially the one she now worked with in the factory. Each day he consumed several glasses of absinthe, but his daily intake also included the local rough red wine and several glasses of brandy. He began to beat her regularly and his sexual advances, although less frequent, became rougher. Fortunately, before her marriage, her mother had told her how to determine when a man's cock could do the most damage, and she had mostly managed to stay out of his way during these fertile periods. But several times he had forced his lust upon her during the danger period, and she had had another child at nineteen. Now she resorted to potions bought from the local quack, and his drinks were always laced with various salts and herbal extracts for at least one week each month. Mercifully, he was usually too drunk to notice her these days, though she was still often on the receiving end of some fearsome beatings.

It was an ugly blue and green facial bruise that she was now holding close to the aperture between her and the priest in their adjacent confessional booths.

"Father - is it a sin to resist my husband's constant demands?"

"My child, you must obey your husband - but he does appear a little forceful."

There was a pause and then a hesitant suggestion:

"Perhaps I should examine your wounds more closely - if I am to speak to your husband. Let us adjourn to my room in the vestry."

The priest was not a stranger to temptations of the flesh - his calling required a total abstinence from thoughts and deeds that most men took for their right. It was a hard cross to bear: the angelic boys of the choir, the doe-eyed maidens in their Sunday best, and the tales of lust and depravity heard in the confessional. Now this pretty mother of two was baring her arm to reveal more of these fearsome green bruises.

"And there's more father," and she pulled up her skirt revealing a long black bruise, red at the edges extending all the way up her thigh to her drawers, and there he glimpsed just a hint of pubic hair.

Without thinking, the blood pounding in his temples, the priest laid his hand on the bruise. There was a sudden disturbance at the vestry door and light flooded into the dimly-lit room

"Oh Father - sorry to disturb you - but remember you agreed to see me to discuss the land that Pernod wants to buy." The hand was withdrawn in a flash, but he knew that Eustace de Séverin, appearing from nowhere, had observed his indiscretion.

"Er yes - we must talk - now say three 'Hail Marys' Madame La Fosse, and I will talk to your husband after Mass."

Florence quickly left the room and Eustace moved in very close to the priest.

"Father – have you considered Pernod's very generous offer for the church lands – it could be very advantageous to both of you?"

"Well – I really should consult with the members of the Church Council."

Eustace sighed and nodded his head gravely.

"Now you wouldn't want the Council to learn of your little indiscretion with Madame La Fosse…"

The priest spluttered. "But that was absolutely nothing – she was merely showing me her bruises."

"And if we're talking about bruises – what about Maurice – that pretty little choir boy. *Mon Dieu* you should see the bruises on his little cock!"

Now it was the turn of the priest to sigh. Life was so unfair.

"Very well – you have my agreement."

★ ★ ★ ★ ★

Eustace de Séverin had led a charmed life. His wealthy parents had ensured that he received the best education that money could buy – firstly at the best local lycée and then at the Sorbonne. They hoped that he would participate in the family business – they were purveyors of fine food and wines; but this was too dull for Eustace and he studied for his articles as a notary public. This appealed to him as an easy option – a licence to print money, especially in a small town. And so it had proved. His life in Pontarlier could not have been better. The almost daily dealings with the recently bereaved, who were grateful for his sympathetic attention and then generous with their payments for his services. Several of the wealthy young widows had also succumbed to his sexual advances as an extra mark of their gratitude for his sympathetic attentions. He was, after all, a handsome young man with considerable charm. This very day, after he completed his dealings with Pernod, he hoped to seduce the young absinthe bottler, Florence La Fosse; but if that failed, there was a rich new widow to visit that evening.

He was waiting for Florence at the corner of the factory, a picnic hamper over his arm.

"Come Madame La Fosse, I have some fine ham and a good red wine in my basket - and some gold napoleons too. Here, take my arm."

And so it was that Jean La Fosse, on his third absinthe, saw Florence and Eustace walk across the square in Pontarlier on the way to their destiny. While Jean was persuaded to stay for further alcohol, his wife and the notary crossed into the river meadow and ate their meal in the shade of a large weeping willow, spangles of bright light shimmering on the surface of the river beside them. The ham was excellent and the strong red wine went straight to Florence's head. She had not intended to drink it,, because she knew the effect it would have. Now, lying replete and slightly tipsy in the dappled shade, she tried to resist as Eustace kissed her gently and his hand moved under her skirt, but the heat and the wine and the sudden pleasure as his fingers sought out her intimate parts were just too much to resist.

After their lovemaking, they both slept for a while, then Eustace lifted her to her feet and kissed her tenderly.

"*C'était merveilleux. Pour tu aussi?*"

She nodded shyly and squeezed him tightly.

"Come, let me walk with to your cottage and you can hide your money from that husband of yours."

★ ★ ★ ★ ★

Jean La Fosse had not returned to the hayloft. After five absinthes he was not in a fit state for anything much, certainly not physical labour. He crossed the fields that separated the village from his cottage. Above him a lone kite soared and wheeled as it scoured the hillsides for prey. His children were staying with their grandparents - an annual treat at this time of year - which meant the cottage was empty. Or was it? Jean thought not.

He entered the cottage as stealthily as his inebriation would allow. His old Vetterli rifle - a souvenir from his days as a legionnaire - hung over the door. He carefully lifted it down and worked the bolt to insert a cartridge into the breech - the magazine was always kept loaded. The stairs creaked with age as he lumbered clumsily towards the upper floor of the cottage. The alcohol from five absinthes had permeated every part of his body, and although his limbs seemed heavy and ungainly, and his vision was blurred, but somehow his mind was clearly focused on what had to be done.

He reached the bedroom door and quietly raised the latch. The scene before him was what he had expected. The sun shone strongly into the room and the motes of dust spiralled slowly downwards through the sunbeams and onto the naked bodies entwined on the bed. The bodies of his wife and the notary - dozing peacefully, exhausted by their exertions and enjoying the warm glow of sexual satisfaction.

So it was true! He was filled with a terrible rage - how could she cheat on him with this young upstart from Paris, just because he was young and rich and... his stomach churned and the bitter after-taste of absinthe rose in his throat. Anger boiled over into hatred, lust, and a desire for terrible revenge. He raised the old Vetterli rifle and fired once and then twice and again and again until he had poured eleven bullets into their bodies, wrenching the bolt action backwards and forwards in time with the leaping of the bodies as each bullet ploughed into their naked forms. Then, slowly and deliberately, he loaded the last cartridge into the breech, turned the rifle around until he could bite upon the muzzle, and pulled the trigger one last time.

Drugs for all reasons

"Right – take down your pants and let's have a look."

No, I hadn't got lucky and some gorgeous girl was after my body. My right testicle was as hard as a rock, and after several sleepless nights I had sought medical advice. Possible diagnoses were not hard to formulate and they were mostly terrifying, but I refused to believe that it could happen to me.

"It is a bit craggy – you might have to lose it" said the doc. There it was. He had voiced the one eventuality I had refused to contemplate. "Though it might just be calcium deposits." A glimmer of hope – I didn't want to lose a 25-year old testicle.

"Take this form to the X-ray Department in the Hospital and I will organise a bed for you as soon as possible." I didn't like the urgency of the ASAP. "It's probably something benign," he suggested as he handed me the form.

I pulled up my underpants and climbed into my trousers. I was only too eager to accept this relatively innocuous possibility, and tried to blank out the alternatives.

At the University Hospital, they X-rayed my chest and abdomen, booked me a bed and said I could go back to work. I walked across Harvard Yard, avoiding the large irregular piles of last Friday's snow, now blackened and frozen solid awaiting the spring or an unseasonable thaw. The Chemistry Department was like a furnace as usual and the intense cold outside (the radio had said ten below) was soon forgotten, but not my depression.

I tried to work in order to forget. I set up my apparatus and charged the round-bottomed flask with magnesium turnings and dry ether, ready for a Grignard reaction. I reached into the fume cupboard for the bottle of bromobenzene, caught my sleeve on the tip of the metal clampstand and pulled the whole thing over, causing the flask to smash on the concrete base of the cupboard. The crash and my swearing brought Donna Stein running in from the next lab.

"Jeez, is that you breaking up the place again? You're one helluva clumsy guy!" she protested. My clumsiness was almost as legendary as Donna's alleged sexual appetite, though she had never made any advances on me, why should she – everyone assumed I was still happily married. My gloom intensified; a broken marriage and soon down to a single ball.

Donna seemed to notice my air of despondency. "Hey you OK? You seem kinda low, wife keep you up late? "

"No, I haven't seen Stella for weeks."

"Huh?"

"She's gone back to England."

Did I want to air my dirty laundry in public after keeping it all quiet so far? Why bore others with my problems? But then I was tired of all the pretence and always lying about our relationship.

"We're separated, it wasn't working for us." There was a glimmer of something on her face; shock, surprise, casual interest? I couldn't decide. Finally she found the words: "I'm sorry, how long?"

"Two months, end of January, but it had been coming on for a long time." And as an afterthought: "The Californian syndrome - too much booze, too many parties and one night on the tiles, instantly regretted."

"Did Stella find out?"

"No, but my guilty conscience made things awkward between us, and she guessed in the end."

A moment's awkward silence and then: "D'you miss her? I'm sorry, that's a stoopid question." She turned to leave, then almost as an aside, as if expecting me to refuse, she asked: "Want to eat at my place tonight?"

"Yeah, that would be nice, what time?"

"Oh about eight, it'll only be pizza, I don't run to that Julia Child haute cuisine stuff."

"Pizza sounds fine, I'll bring a bottle of plonk."

"Sounds disgusting, you English and your silly words (she put on her best English accent), sponge bag, petrol, perambulator, jeez!"

"God that's rich, coming from a Yank, you're the ones who have corrupted the Queen's English!"

Further discussion was cut short by the appearance of our boss, Professor Brockhaven, scourge of us all and ready for his daily progress report. His crewcut and carefully clipped moustache were reminders of his days as a conscript in Vietnam, a huge waste of his time and intellect (as he was often reminding us), but an experience that had endowed him with a lack of patience for those less able than himself, and (as one of the other postdocs had so perceptively observed) a ramrod up his arse.

The broken glass crunched under his feet as he entered the lab and he half-sneered in Donna's direction: "Another bit of English carelessness, like the loss of the Colonies." The sneer turned into a weak smile; he was evidently pleased with his joke. He asked me about my experiments, but I had little to tell him and he turned on his heel, promising to return later for a more lengthy discussion and a list of experiments for me to try, I could count on that.

He hadn't reappeared by 5.30, so I slunk off via the back door and went first to the liquor store for a large bottle of Californian burgundy, then home for a wash and change. My two-room apartment was very modest, a living room-cum-kitchen and a bedroom, but at least the heating came with the $80 a month rent, and it was close to the lab. I shaved and showered more to remove the stink of the lab than to get prepared for an evening of seduction. I can't pretend that I hadn't considered the possibility of sex with Donna, who certainly had a reputation for one-night stands, but I was still very preoccupied with my right testicle and the prospect of losing it.

Donna's place was much more salubrious than mine, and she even had a separate kitchen and her own bathroom, I shared one with five others. Her father was a lawyer and she had gained her first degree from Radcliffe before embarking on a PhD in Chemistry at Harvard.

"Hi, you found the place then, come in" she said at the door. She seemed very cheery and had changed out of her scruffy, acid-holed jeans into a pair of green dungarees and a T shirt which declared 'RADCLIFFE GIRLS ARE ALWAYS ON TOP'.

"Something smells good."

"Cheese and pepperoni pizza, hope you'll like it."

"Absolutely no doubt, have you got a corkscrew? I'll pour us some vino."

"In the drawer next to the freezer, I'll just go and finish fixing the table."

I located the corkscrew, pulled the cork and poured the cheap but pleasantly aromatic red wine into the two glasses she'd left on the kitchen table. I carried them into her living room and set them down on the table, which bore a red check tablecloth, expensive-looking cutlery and some plates that were certainly English china. I raised my glass.

"Cheers, and thanks for the invite, I was feeling a bit low this afternoon."

"Cheers, you're welcome, any time. Hey that's nice wine,

I usually drink beer or coke, so this is a real treat."

"I was going to splash out on some French stuff, I expect you're used to that at home."

"Not likely, Daddy won't have foreign wine in the house, he's very patriotic. Puts out the flag on July 4th and Thanksgiving, even sometimes on Mothers' Day!" She laughed. "Last of the big-time flag-wavers is Daddy, fought for his country in the last war, would have gone to Vietnam if he hadn't been too old. He has no time for Spics, Krauts, Russkies, Japs or Chinks, thinks they're all troublemakers living off the benevolence of the good ole US of A."

She drained her glass. "I guess we can eat. Bring your glass, because I'm a little short after my last party." The pizza was hot in both senses, and delicious. We ate and drank and talked, mostly about nothing in particular: work, getting a real job, the weather, skiing (she'd just come back from a long weekend in Vermont), mutual friends and who was sleeping with who.

We finished the bottle of wine over cheese and biscuits and she brought out a bottle of cheap Mexican brandy she'd bought on her previous vacation to Acapulco. Skiing in Vermont and sunning in Acapulco, the life of a rich Radcliffe girl. I was beginning to feel quite pissed, my words sliding and slithering together. She obviously felt the same.

"You're pished" she suggested.

"You sound pretty far gone yourself."

"Let's go to bed."

Even in my inebriated state, this came as something of a

surprise, but a not unwelcome one, and without further formalities we headed for the bedroom, shedding clothes on the way. She worked at my belt buckle while I fumbled with her bra, never my strong point; she laughed at me hopping on one leg and tugging at the sock on the other foot. But finally, after much fumbling and grappling, we were both out of our underwear and into action.

My performance was poor - perhaps it was the booze or a full stomach, or maybe my craggy testicle let me down, who knows - but she didn't seem to mind and afterwards we slept, still entwined. A cold, grey dawn outside, and inside, crumpled bedclothes and the odour of alcohol, sweat and semen, and in the pit of my stomach a tight knot of fear. Friday's operation loomed ever nearer.

Donna stirred beside me, but my desire for sex had evaporated and I knew that my early morning breath would be a complete turn-off. I got up and showered, then gathered up my crumpled street clothes, which formed a trail to the bedroom. It seemed rude to go before she awoke, so I made us both some coffee and toast and carried it into the bedroom.

"Your breakfast Mademoiselle, did you also want the morning paper?"

"Mmmm, that would be nice, and perhaps a freshly squeezed orange."

"I'll see what I can find." I rose from the bed to go to the kitchen.

"Only joking, but hey this is real nice."

We ate and drank in silence. She seemed much smaller and

less imposing with a sheet wrapped around her. I began to realise that a lot of her appeal came from her expensive clothes and hairdos. Without her clothes and makeup she was not a patch on Stella, who looked so good both in and out of her clothes, most of which she made herself. I felt tears of self-pity welling up in my eyes; time to leave and face grim reality.

In a funny sado-masochistic sort of way, I enjoy the total oblivion of surgical operations. The total blank between the anaesthetist's needle and the painless torpor in the recovery room. The instantaneous progression from one ceiling and set of lights to the next. I had heard that they pinch your earlobe to bring you back to consciousness, but I have never felt it.

The surgeon had said: "Of course you realise we can't open your scrotum just to have a look, we'll have to remove the testicle." So out it came via a three-inch incision just above and to the right of my penis. I apparently caused a slight upset when I arrived in theatre with a full growth of pubic hair – well, no one had told me to remove it - and some poor nurse probably got a bollocking.

Safely back in my room, I dared not feel for the stitches. I drifted into and out of slumber while the anaesthetic slowly lost it grip. In the evening, I felt fine. I had some peanut and jelly sandwiches, then plucked up the courage to examine my scrotum. It seemed almost the same size as before, though somewhat withered and slightly numb, but at least one ball remained intact. "You'll fire perfectly well on one cylinder," they had told me, though I was in no hurry to prove them right.

I slept soundly through the night, glad the initial trauma was over. Next morning I eagerly awaited the doctor's visit and what I hoped would be a speedy release from hospital. Instead he asked: "Have you ever had TB?"

At first the question seemed so unrelated to my present condition that I could not see the awful implication that lay behind his question. I assured him that I had not had TB.

"Something showed up on your chest X-ray."

An iron hand seemed to grip my intestines and I am sure that I turned very pale.

"We shall have to wait for the histology report on the testicle, but I'm afraid that it likely to show a malignant teratoma."

"What's that?

"It's a piece of embryonic tissue that starts to grow, and of course it shouldn't now that you're an adult. Have you been kicked in the testicles recently?"

I shook my head.

"Well its starts to grow very rapidly, and sometimes the malignant cells break away and form colonies elsewhere in the body, often in the lungs."

He looked at me intently, trying to gauge how I was taking the news.

"And that's what you believe has happened?" I asked weakly.

"I'm afraid so, but let's wait for the histology report before we jump to too many conclusions. OK?"

I nodded weakly, my heart in my boots, my guts in a

tangle. He'd been very blunt. To think that yesterday I had been worried about losing a ball, and today I probably had lung cancer! The sudden twists and turns of fate.

The doctor departed, his bombshell delivered; the patient left to his own thoughts of mortality. I thought of Stella and tears welled up in my eyes. Death is such a final thing and I was suddenly full of self-pity: people and things seen, held, smelt, tasted, loved, hated, never to be experienced again.

Yet now a mechanism for self-preservation swung into effect and I quickly convinced myself that the lung spot would be an old TB scar, long forgotten; hadn't my mother talked about a bad attack of a whooping-cough-like illness when I was five? Optimism and positive thinking bring with them a warm glow and an instant recovery of spirits. But my optimism was unjustified. When I returned some days later for the histology report, it was all bad news. It was indeed a malignant teratoma, and there was a strong suspicion that the lung shadow was a secondary deposit.

"I'm going to recommend that you return to England for treatment," my surgeon suggested. "We could treat you here, but even with Blue Cross insurance it's going to be very expensive, and to be quite honest the specialist centres in Britain are just as good as ours for this type of cancer."

The cold hand of fear again. "What is the treatment?"

"Well, here we would probably carry out a lobectomy, that's removal of the damaged bit of lung, but your doctors are much more conservative and have this new regime of chemotherapy coupled with radiotherapy. It won't be pleasant, but they are having some good successes."

"So what should I do?"

"I have a colleague, Ethan Cohen, who's on a year's sabbatical at the Royal Cancer Hospital just outside of Reading." (He pronounced it Reeding, but I knew where he meant.) "I can give you a letter of introduction and I'm sure they will see you. They need as many patients as possible who are newly diagnosed so that they can measure the success of their treatment."

I wasn't sure I fancied the idea of being a guinea pig, but Reading was where my parents lived, so at least I would have a place to stay. Who knows, if I contacted Stella she might forgive my past transgressions now that I was seriously ill. My capacity for self-pity and optimism knew no bounds.

So a week later, with stitches removed and my remaining testicle apparently undamaged, I packed and said my farewells. Professor Brockhaven was pretty reasonable about the whole thing, even somewhat distressed, and offered to act as a referee should I need one.

Donna was the only one who knew what had happened and I hoped she would be discreet. She was very upset for me and even suggested a final sexual fling, a kind of before-and-after exercise. I was tempted, but declined her offer, more out of fear of failure than anything else.

I rang my mother.

"Mum, it's me, Marty."

She was evidently surprised. "Marty? Is anything wrong? Are you OK?"

I suddenly lost my nerve and couldn't tell her over the

phone. "I'm coming home, back to England, next Tuesday."

"That's lovely, but why? This is so sudden."

"Oh nothing much, I'll explain when I see you. Can you meet me at the airport, I'll have quite a lot of luggage?"

A moment's hesitation. "Well your father will have to have the day off, but he's got a few days owing in lieu so that should be all right."

"Thanks, my flight gets into Heathrow at 12 noon, it's BA 374."

And that was that, all arranged and the pips for three minutes went as I put the phone down. England sounded very close.

The family reunion at Heathrow was pretty emotional. My mother and sister cried, and my father shook my hand, a sure sign of deep emotion. But behind the smiles and tears lay doubt; they were bursting to ask all kinds of questions.

Once safely in the car and on the M4, I broke the news about my teratoma. They listened in silence until I had finished, then my father asked one of his inane questions: "Will you still be able to...?"

He paused, probably remembering that having broken up with Stella, my sex life might be non-existent anyway.

"Yes Dad, I will, or so they tell me, firing on one cylinder."

He seemed relieved. Of course, his generation had been brought up to worry about manhood and virility.

"What about the spot on your lung Marty?"

My sister was a hospital dietician and so was a bit more knowledgeable than my parents about medical matters.

"I don't know, but knowing my luck it's probably rather serious. I'll find out on Monday when I go to hospital."

That was that. I asked after Stella, but no one had seen her or heard from her since she returned to England. Both sets of parents seemed to have declared a mutual excommunication, apparently each blaming the other side's offspring for the break-up. I could well believe that my mother would find it inconceivable that her darling Marty could chase after other women. And Stella's parents would have heard about my wicked behaviour from her, and would have probably told her that they were not surprised given their general animosity towards me. After all I had got their dear daughter pregnant out of wedlock, and if it hadn't been for a miscarriage after ten weeks, she would have gone to the altar with a bump in her wedding dress. Stella's mother had greeted the news of the foetal loss with a 'perhaps it's for the best dear', which had not been well received, since Stella had begun to get quite excited about being a mother.

The weekend passed quickly and I was totally pampered: breakfast in bed, lunch in the garden, tea in front of the TV. My mother bought me new towels, flannels and pyjamas, the best that M&S could provide, and laden with all this new apparel, together with chocolate biscuits, fruit and squash, I arrived at the Royal Cancer Hospital the following Monday morning.

The buildings were new, pleasant to look at, and surrounded by extensive and well-stocked gardens. Overall it looked a bit like a Costa Brava hotel, but without the sun and the beach. My letter of appointment directed me to the Radiography Department, where I was to have a lymphangiogram. I had a rough idea what they were going to do, so I wasn't alarmed when my feet were anaesthetised, then injected with blue dye to visualise my lymphatics.

The woman doctor was very proficient and quickly located the lymph vessels she wanted to study. Then she inserted thin plastic catheters before injecting me with iodine in sesame oil. She sent me for a brief walk around so that the iodine would spill over into lymphatics above my waistline.

We chatted while she was taking X-rays of my lymph system. She had trained in Glasgow, had hated Chemistry, which she found irrelevant to her medical course, and had found the culture of booze and brawling that was prevalent in the City both exhilarating and somewhat frightening. She found life in Reading rather tame in comparison..

I was released from Radiography and told to find my way to Chester-Beatty ward, which was to be my home for the duration of my treatment. The ward comprised male and female rooms and a large central 'play area' complete with snooker table and several ping pong tables. This area was neatly bisected by a row of armchairs, which allowed for a very effective segregation of the sexes: on their side the women knitted and nattered, comparing (so I discovered) weights, pains and various other gripes, while on the male side there was incessant playing of snooker and table tennis.

A rather charming Oriental nurse showed me to my bed, deep in the male preserve and one of six in a pleasant brightly-lit room. I had a simple divan bed, a chest of drawers, a built-in wardrobe and a console comprising radio, light and a nurse-call button. One man lay sleeping attached to a drip stand.

"The doctor will probably come and see you later," she told me.

"Should I change into my pyjamas?"

She laughed. "No, not unless you want to, the lads usually wear normal clothes during the day, unless they are having treatment."

I unpacked my few bits and stowed them in the chest of drawers, then found the toilets for a pee. I was taken aback to find that it was aquamarine in colour, but realised that this must be the dye emerging from my body.

I wandered into the main room and found an armchair on the male side of the divide. I had brought along my copy of Lord of the Rings, which I had been reserving for my next long holiday, though my present incarceration was not quite what I had had in mind as a background to the tale of hobbits and wizards.

No one spoke to me, and I didn't feel like making an effort myself. Quite a few of the patients in the room were either bald or nearly hairless, though the women tended to cover their baldness with headscarves. I hoped that I wouldn't get the type of drugs that caused such awful hair loss.

Dr Cohen materialised soon after and immediately identified me as a new patient. "Marty Sloman?"

I nodded, and he indicated that I was to accompany him

to my bed for an examination. He was short and quite rounded in the middle and seemed a bit abrupt at first.

"Strip to your underpants please and lie on the bed" he ordered. I stripped to my M&S floral pants (my mother's idea of a Christmas joke) and lay on the bed. He felt my remaining testicle, pressed various parts of my abdomen, listened to my chest, and looked in my eyes.

"OK, you can get dressed" he said. He sat on my bed writing notes in a large notebook. "How much do you know about your condition?"

"In the US my doctor, your colleague, told me he had removed a malignant teratoma and that there was a chance I had a secondary deposit in my right lung."

"And you're a chemist, so I guess you will have looked up teratoma in the medical books."

I had done a bit of reading in Harvard Library, but it had all been so depressing, survival chances around 10%.

"Yes I did do a bit of reading, but all the books were at least five years out of date. They were also pretty depressing, saying that teratoma was resistant to drugs and radiotherapy."

"Yes, well you're right the books are usually not very helpful, the situation has changed very recently with the introduction of some new drugs."

I felt relieved, but not for long.

"I won't disguise the seriousness of the situation, but let's be optimistic. Now this afternoon we'll give you an IVP, it's a procedure that allows us to look at your waterworks, then an ultrasound of your abdomen."

I must have looked a bit concerned, because he sought to reassure me. "None of that will be unpleasant, just a lot of lying around on couches. Then tomorrow the consultant will see you to discuss what is to be done. All right?"

I nodded.

"OK, I'll see you again tomorrow," and then as an afterthought, "Try not to worry, we've had some good success lately."

And with that he got off the bed and was gone from the room.

Lunch arrived soon after. The food was fair but the presentation was poor; you had to help yourself from a heated trolley that smelt of stale, warmed-up meals. In the beginning, before the drugs sapped my strength, I ate voraciously, but as the weeks dragged on, I ate less and less, and the sight and smell of the trolley eventually induced a feeling of nausea as surely as the bells that induced Pavlov's dogs to salivate.

After lunch I was summoned for my IVP, which was quick but unpleasant: 10ml of saline and iodine injected intravenously by a consultant who obviously used a needle very rarely. It hurt like hell as he probed around to find a vein, then stabbed me.

"You'll notice a warm feeling in a moment, perhaps a salty taste in your mouth" he said. With that, his work done, he fled the scene, leaving me with an overwhelming desire to vomit, but by the time the radiologist had grabbed a bowl in response to my gagging noises, the feeling had passed.

The rest was easy and I just lay back while they took X-rays every ten minutes or so. The ultrasound was really pleasant. An oily abdomen and a sound source which felt like a small rubber ball, rolling back and forth while the technician peeled off black and white pictures of my insides.

"Can I have a copy?" I asked.

"You wouldn't understand it." Yes, but it might look nice on my bedroom wall.

I arrived back on the ward just in time to hear a dear old lady (she looked over 70) telling the other ladies of her recent trauma in the X-ray department.

"I went for me X-ray, and you know they tell you to strip and put on a gown." Nods from the assembled knitters and natterers. "Well how was I to know you was supposed to keep yer knickers on?" Wry smiles from the women. "The wretched girl laughed at me and asked me if I was planning a floor show. Damn cheek!" More smiles and much sympathetic head shaking.

In the evening after supper, those of the lads who were well enough went out to the pub. They asked me if I wanted to join them, but I was feeling rather low, so I elected to stay on the ward. In reality I was taken by surprise, not expecting any hospital to operate an open-door policy. However, when I thought about it I realised that since the life expectancy of many of the patients was likely to be short, no one was going to stop the lads going out for a few beers and a game of darts.

My evening in also allowed me to explore the ward. It was by now clear that this was a treatment ward with very little general nursing activity. Evidently people took to their beds for their chemotherapy and subsequent recovery, and apart from that they were free to come and go more or less at will. There was a large TV room, and I spent some time trying to find something worth watching, but I was eventually distracted around eight o'clock by the arrival of a very cheery night nurse.

"Hi, are you our new boy?" she asked, peering into the TV room. "I'm Jan, d'you want to take charge of milky drinks?"

I must have looked a bit vacant, so she explained. "Since you're new and so far drug free, I thought you might feel like helping."

I got out of the chair. "Yes of course, I'd be very happy to help."

"Great, let me show you where everything is."

We went off to the kitchen and she showed me the tins of Horlicks, Bournvita, drinking chocolate, tea and coffee and rows of coloured mugs in the wall cupboard.

"Just boil up loads of milk on the gas ring and put it into those big insulated jugs, then wheel the trolley round the ward and give people what they want. OK? It's easy."

It was, and quite good fun too, at least it kept me from brooding about the next day. All my fellow patients were suitably grateful, though I now noted that many of them had their heads in their hands, obviously tired and perhaps low at the end of the day.

I finished my dispensing just as the lads came in from the pub. They were quite noisy and Jan came bustling out of one of the side wards to admonish them.

"Come on you rowdy bunch, quieten down and get yourselves ready for bed. Then I can come and tuck you in." Typical male innuendo followed: "Yes miss, I might need help with my buttons." "Will you be getting in with me tonight Jan?"

She bustled off to see to a patient who had just rung his or her bell. I had to admit, she was really nice. She was pretty in a homely way and appeared cuddly, with a round cherubic face and a deep dimple in her chin. I looked forward to being tucked in, but in the event I was so tired from the day's events that I was asleep before she came on her ward round.

I slept surprisingly well and ate a huge breakfast, almost for the last time. At around ten I was summoned to the examination suite on the first floor and, as usual, asked to strip to pants and socks. I sat on the bed in a small chilly room, goose pimples emerging all over my body. And that's the way I stayed for about half an hour, getting more and more nervous and irritated all the time.

Suddenly a gust of wind blew open the door and exposed me to the fully dressed patients who were sitting outside in the waiting area. We were all embarrassed and I rushed over and closed the door just before a Scottish voice enquired: "Where have you put Mr Sloman?" A nurse peered round the door. "He's in here Professor McRob."

The Professor, a tall, imposing man in a smart grey business suit, entered the room, followed by his entourage of housemen and Dr Cohen. He shook my hand vigorously. "Sorry to keep you waiting so long. Lie back on the bed please." Then he proceeded to poke and feel me in all the places Cohen had probed the day before. He then held up the various X-rays and peered at them.

"Dr Cohen tells me that you are aware of the serious nature of your condition."

I nodded.

"You definitely have a spot of cancer here." He tapped me on the chest just about my right nipple. "We think you have a small abdominal abnormality as well." He paused to let the news sink in. "We are going to attack the cancer vigorously with drugs, then give you a course of radiotherapy, then some more drugs. It won't be pleasant and I can't make any promises about the outcome. However, we have had some successes recently, and it has been with patients like you who have been apparently healthy with just one or two small lesions."

He waited again for my reactions, but what could I say?

"Have you any questions?"

"Well, I am a chemist, so I'm interested in what type of drugs you are going to give me."

"OK, fair enough. First of all we're going to give you a drug called cyclophosphamide."

I groaned audibly, I knew all about that one.

"I'm afraid you're going to lose all of your hair. You can have a wig if you wish. After cyclophosphamide, it will depend on how you are responding to the treatment. Any other questions?"

I couldn't think of any, apart from: "If I refused treatment, not of course that I'm going to, how long would I last?"

"I think you would be lucky to last two years, probably less."

So with treatment I should last beyond my 25th birthday! Suddenly that seemed like an eternity, and I felt cheered.

"I'm sure that you will think of lots of other questions, so don't hesitate to ask Dr Cohen, who will be in charge of your day-to-day treatment. I will see you every Monday on my ward round."

And that was that. The future was mapped out for me; several months of misery, then perhaps normality. At least I felt a bit more optimistic.

Chemotherapy began with a vengeance the next day. First of all I had an early trip to the urogenital department, where they filled me full of radioactive chromium, then watched it come back out, and so established that my kidneys could take the strain. Then back to my bed for the treatment.

"Take these then get into bed." The rather severe ward sister proffered two chlorpromazine pills.

"What are they for?" I enquired somewhat naively.

"Anti-sickness pills, just like you take if you are going on a boat trip, but stronger."

I swallowed, took a gulp of water, then lay on the bed., nervous but also excited, the thrill of the unknown.

"Have you ever had one of these?" A very pretty and deeply suntanned Australian nurse held up a drip set. I soon learnt that she was one of two drug administrators on the ward.

"No."

"Well there's nothing to it. Are you right-handed?" I nodded. "Right I'll put the stand here and connect you up." She was indicating the left side of the bed. I rolled up my left pyjama sleeve and rested my arm on the pillow she had placed on the edge of the bed. She applied a tourniquet, found a vein on the back of my left wrist, swabbed it with ether, then said "sharp prick" And there was. Like a needle travelling the length of my arm.

"Jeez, what tough skin, but I'm in." She manoeuvred the needle until its entire length was immersed in the vein, then connected me to the drip set.

"Did they tell you what you're having?" she asked.

"Cyclophosphamide."

"Well, they've changed their minds, you're really lucky, you are getting this new platinum drug instead, we've only just got the supply in this morning."

It seemed that the new drug, technical name cis-dichloro-diammino-platinum (II), was still experimental, but was proving to be very potent at killing teratoma cells. Unfortunately it was hell for the kidneys, like any heavy metal.

"We'll keep you afloat all the while by pumping vast amounts of saline through you, and you'll pee buckets" she said. And I did, 12 full bottles in 25 hours. Oh, and five bowls of vomit, the last one bright green, and all the while I felt as if I was in the grip of the flu.

The day was a blur, and my only recollection, apart from the peeing and the vomiting, was of the first night, when Jan came and put her arm round me on several occasions while I was being particularly vomitous. Her soft warmth and her delicate floral perfume were like a pleasant dream among the continuous nightmares.

Finally it was over and someone came and took the drip away, and after a further day of slipping into and out of sleep, I started to feel a bit better. On the third day I was judged well enough to go home, and my parents came to collect me for a one-week break. My mother spent all week trying to build me up and cheer me up. Huge meals on demand, bars of chocolate *ad libitum* and as much Mackeson stout as I could drink; she'd read in *Woman's Realm* that cancer patients should drink lots of stout, especially Guinness, but she knew I couldn't stand the black stuff. I read the paper and watched lots of TV, and the week was gone in a flash.

All too soon it was time to return to the hospital. They ran an X-ray of my lung and the news was good: the spot was shrinking and they said they were pleased. I was pleased too! Something positive at last.

"We're going to try you on our second drug cocktail," Dr Cohen informed me. "It's a mixture of bleomycin from a Japanese fungus which we'll drip into you for five days, and on days one and five, we'll add some vinblastine."

"I know that one, from the Madagascar periwinkle," I said knowledgeably. "It stops cell division." He grunted assent. Doctors do not like know-it-all patients.

"We'll fit you up with a walking drip-stand so that you can walk around the ward, even play snooker."

For the first two days that is just what I did. I ate, drank, watched TV, read and trundled around the ward, observing my fellow patients. Some did look grim: the ex-military policeman now a mere skeleton; the man with no upper lip who still contrived to smoke; the young woman with a racking cough that made me wince. There were endless arguments over the TV: too loud, wrong channel, no picture, horizontal hold in need of twiddling.

On the third day I took the roof off my mouth with a bag of crisps. The nurse said I had oral thrush and gave me some cream. Then the aches and pains started, and the night sweats left me lying in a pool of water, an experience that felt like childhood bed-wetting. My stomach ached, as did my limbs and head. They gave me strong painkillers, but they barely touched the pain. I did not eat because my mouth and throat were raw, and when I drank the Carnation instant food, I always brought it straight back up.

On day four the doctors came around to see me. I tried to look like death warmed up, which was not difficult. "Don't worry, if you feel so bad, think how the tumour cells must feel" Professor McRob reassured me. But he was very upbeat about the X-ray results and told me to "hang in there".

Finally it was over, though really it was just the beginning. I should have guessed what the sequel would be having talked to some of the other patients, but initially I was just glad to be free of the drip-stand. I bathed and roamed the ward again.

"Your white cell count has dropped a lot," the ward sister informed me. "If it drops any further you might have to go into isolation for a few days." It proceeded to drop right down into my boots, and they shut me away in a private room. I lay on the bed, drank and regurgitated Carnation, sweated all the time and got weaker and weaker.

Then my hair started to fall out. At first a few stray hairs, then fistfuls, and soon the pillow and the rest of the bed were full of them. I felt so ill and miserable. Someone got concerned about my temperature spikes and I had blood cultures done to look for bacterial infection. But mercifully there was none. My blood was checked every morning and lo and behold, the white cell count started to rise, slowly at first but then by leaps and bounds.

Finally Professor McRob said I was well enough to go home, but then I farted and filled my pyjamas. The bleomycin had stopped my digestive system in its tracks, so for two days I had been taking Mil-Par by the glassful, and this had now reversed the constipation in dramatic fashion. I didn't know whether to be relieved or embarrassed. Sister said I couldn't go home in my present state, but I pleaded to be allowed home to the care of my mother, and eventually she relented.

"You've had a battering," Ethan Cohen announced rather unnecessarily. "We'll give you a three-week break, then have you back for some radiotherapy." Something to look forward to.

My father tried hard to disguise his look of horror when he came to collect me. I had lost a stone in weight, most of my hair was gone, and I could hardly stagger to the car. But the cool night air felt so good and my father's strained small talk seemed so fresh.

The resilience of the human body is amazing, and within ten days of getting home, my mother's highly calorific meals had given me back some of the lost weight and lots of new white blood cells. My strength returned and I no longer staggered to and from the bathroom. I even felt like trying the *Telegraph* crossword each day.

Various friends rang to ask after my health and one morning Stella phoned. "How are you?" she asked hesitantly.

"I was pretty grim, but I'm feeling much better now, what about you? What are you up to?"

She had found a job at a primary school near to her parents in Shrewsbury, that was the job she had trained to do. At present she was living with them, though she was looking for somewhere of her own. I told her about my experiences at the Royal Cancer Hospital and joked about my baldness and the long-haired (Beatle mop) wig that had been fitted before leaving the hospital. There was a moment's silence.

"Marty, I've found someone else" she said. There it was. She had dashed my hopes of seeking her forgiveness and asking if we could make a new start.

"Oh" was all I could manage.

"He's one of the other teachers at my school."

"I don't know what to say, I guess I'm very happy for you. I was a real shit and I'm really sorry, but I guess we can't turn the clock back."

"No."

And that was that. We chatted for a few more minutes and agreed that we would talk again about a formal divorce once she'd sorted out her new relationship. A heavy weight hung over me, and I mainly mooched around for the rest of the day. But the next day the hurt was gone and I started to think positively about the future, spurred on by the fact that I had experienced a sudden erection in the middle of going to the loo. My surprise was followed by a surge of real joy. Maybe life wasn't so bad after all.

All too soon my three weeks of rest and recuperation were over and I returned to the Royal Cancer Hospital to face five weeks of daily radiotherapy to my chest and abdomen. They did my front one day and my back the next, with my penis suspended in a leaden cup or enclosed by ponderous lead hemispheres. Disappointingly, the radiographer's cool female fingers somehow managed to manoeuvre the lead without ever touching my penis.

Then I lay alone in the thick-walled room listening to the click of the X-ray machine. I tried so hard to lie still that I got the shakes, and only the thought that the ordeal would only last for five minutes kept me going.

The one advantage of my radiotherapy regime was that it was all over by ten each morning, and the rest of the day was my own. Most days I left the hospital and walked into Reading to look around the shops, or went to the public library to read the daily papers with the old codgers who were usually reading the *Angling Times* or *Railway Modeller.*

On day four I was wandering along the towpath of the Kennet & Avon Canal where it passed through Reading when I saw what I thought was a familiar figure.

"Hey, Jan?"

She turned, and no amount of blusher could disguise the fact that she had a black eye and a bruised cheek.

"Oh, Hi Marty," she said. Her hand rose halfway to her cheek, then she checked herself.

"What's happened to you, that looks painful."

She was quick and had probably been preparing her answer since the 'accident'. "Banged myself on the fridge door, got up too quickly." Then to provide further reassurance. "It's not as bad as it seems."

She was obviously keen to change the subject. "How's your radiotherapy going? I haven't seen you since you went home after your last lot of chemo. You look OK, I like your new hairstyle."

"Yeah, not bad. I didn't know you lived in Reading."

"Yes, we have a small terraced house along here, my partner and I."

The towpath was lined with redbrick two-up two-down Victorian terraced houses, the sort that would have had an outdoor toilet which had now been incorporated into an extension on the kitchen.

"D'you want to come in for a cup of tea?" she asked. "I live just along here."

"Hey, that would be great, let me help you with your bags."

I relieved her of two of her four Sainsbury bags. We reached her house and she rooted in her bag for the door keys and let us in.

"Sorry it's a bit untidy, I only have a few hours each day

to tidy up before night duty" she said. Like most such houses the front door opened straight into the front room, which had a two-seater sofa, an armchair, a TV and old fireplace. An ornament had fallen from the mantelpiece into the hearth and lay smashed, but she didn't seem to notice it and went straight into the kitchen. I followed her and sat on one of the two bar stools at the small table while she filled the kettle. She lit a gas ring of the small cooker then busied herself with two mugs and a box of teabags.

"I've only got PG Tips, that OK?"

"Fine, anything." She looked different in her street clothes and with her hair down. Even nicer than in uniform, her tightish corduroy dungarees made her seem less rounded, and I could see that she had a really nice figure.

"Why do you do night duty all the time?" I asked.

"Oh, it's more convenient, my partner works nights too."

"What does he do?"

A moment's hesitation. "He works in one of clubs in town, part-time bouncer and part-time barman."

The kettle boiled and she prepared the mugs of tea.

"We can sit here in the kitchen. D'you want a digestive? Not much else I'm afraid."

"A digestive would be fine."

She handed me my tea and proffered a round biscuit barrel.

"So how did you come to work at the Royal Cancer Hospital?"

"Well, after school I went to London to do my basic nurse

training, then after my SRN I spent some time specialising at the Royal Marsden in Sutton."

"Why cancer? You must find it very depressing seeing lots of patients die."

She laughed. "Oh you'd be surprised, yes people do die but somehow there's this indomitable spirit, especially on Chester-Beatty ward. The lads make me laugh because no matter how ill they are they can still come out with innuendos and sexist remarks, and some people do actually get better. The new drugs and the other treatments really are making a difference." Suddenly she was quite passionate. "It's especially exciting with teratoma patients like you. A couple of years ago they mostly came in to die, now many of them are being cured, or apparently so, it's too soon to know for sure." She grinned at me. "And on top of that, I like being in charge at night, and being the angel of mercy. Gives me a nice warm feeling."

I felt a warm glow of affection for her. "Now what about you?" she asked. "What were you doing before you got the teratoma?"

What should I tell her? Everything, I supposed.

"Well, I did my BSc and PhD in London, then went to the States to do some research." I took a breath. "Got married at 22 and two years later I was stupid, I had a couple of one-night stands. My wife found out and now we're getting a divorce, she's found someone else."

"Oh, I'm sorry, I didn't mean to pry."

"It's OK, it was all my fault, a couple of acts of stupidity, balls bigger than my brain, though one of them has now paid the price!"

She laughed again. "Well, the other one will live to fight another day."

"I had my first erection the other day" I said. I instantly regretted my familiarity with her. I think I blushed.

"Well that's great news" she said. "We'll have you fighting fit and shagging again in no time!"

There was no time to be surprised or respond to her candour because then there was the sound of a key in the lock, and the front door burst open. A short but muscular man with a crewcut came into the house. It was obvious that this was the partner, because he took one look at the pair of us and rushed at me, grabbing me by the arm and propelling me towards the front door.

"I don't know what the fuck you're doing here pal, but you ain't staying!" he growled. He was much stronger than me, and despite my protests and reassurance from Jan that I was a patient on her ward, within seconds the front door had been opened and I was in a heap on the towpath.

The door slammed behind me and there were shouts from within. I got to my feet and banged at the front door knocker. "Bugger off if you don't want yer skull crushed!" the man shouted.

I slunk off, a cowardly act, but what could I do? He was her partner and I had already ruined one relationship.

Back at the hospital I spent a miserable afternoon, racked with doubt. Should I have made more effort? It didn't seem like much of a relationship. I was fairly sure now that her bruises had been caused by something other than a fridge door. But it was too late now.

I waited anxiously for her to arrive for night duty. Eight o'clock came and went and she did not appear. When a new night nurse turned up in her place, I asked if she knew where Jan was. Apparently she had phoned in sick.

That made me very worried indeed. I slept badly and felt gloomy in the morning, though my mood was improved after breakfast when, unexpectedly, Dr Cohen came on to the ward and sought me out.

"Good news," he declared, waving an X-ray at me (from yesterday I imagined). "Your latest pictures are looking great. No sign of any tumour in the lung. The drugs have really clobbered the cells. Well done, hang in there."

I felt elated as I went down for my daily dose of X-rays, but lying there listening to the click of the machine and trying not to shake too much, my mind returned to Jan and her bruises. After I was released I decided to go and see her, hoping desperately that her partner was out, though I was determined to try and stand up to him if he was at home.

I knocked somewhat tentatively at her door and for several minutes there was no response. I banged a bit more forcefully, and this time the door opened.

She looked dreadful. The side of her face was now a mass of bruises, and she looked dishevelled in her nightie and dressing gown.

"Jeez what has that bastard done to you!"

"You'd better go away, he'll kill you if he finds you here."

But I wasn't going. "No, this is not acceptable, what the hell is going on? Why's he beating you?"

"OK come in, but only for a minute."

We sat on her sofa. I wanted to put my arm around her, but held back in case he suddenly appeared.

"Come on, tell me what's going on" I said. She began to weep, and then I did put my arm around her. Between sobs she told me about the drugs she had taken from the ward for him to sell in the Reading clubs. They were mostly heroin and some benodiazepines. I asked her why. What kind of hold could this violent bastard have over her? She told me how they had met at a club when she first came to Reading. At first he had been kind and attentive, even charming and funny. She had fallen for him, and they moved into the house together, but then she needed money and he lent her some, quite a lot in fact, and it had seemed so easy to steal drugs to pay him back. But in the past few weeks it had got harder to get the drugs, and the beatings had begun.

Now she broke down altogether and sobbed uncontrollably. I took her in my arms and gave her the tightest hug possible.

And then, of course, the bastard came thundering through the door. I had been stupid to come, for both of us. He raged at us, his face crimson as he pushed me aside and grabbed Jan by the hair. His arms flailed wildly as he beat her about the head and body and she finally slumped to the floor.

Then he turned to me. "Right wanker, it's your turn." He

grabbed me round the neck and held me in a full armlock while I tried desperately to knee him in the balls. He began to punch me in the face, and I felt my nose crumple and begin to bleed profusely, but just as I felt that my time was up there was a loud clang. The strength went out of his body as he slowly crumpled to the floor.

I looked up to see Jan standing there with a very large cast-iron frying pan.

"Wow, thanks!" was all I could manage, as I felt for my nose to try and staunch the flow of blood. Jan went to the kitchen and returned with a roll of kitchen towel. She dabbed gently at my nose and face.

"Now we both look a mess" she said, and suddenly she laughed and gave me a huge kiss full on the lips,

"I really enjoyed that, the bastard had that coming" she said. "I'm going to call the police and get all of this off my chest."

She knelt down beside me and offered me some more paper towels. "Will you help me, be a sort of character witness?"

"You bet. For another kiss I'll say anything you like." We kissed again.

"I hope that won't be necessary, just some honest support."

My heart swelled with warmth for her.

The police, when they arrived were only too delighted to have a reason to arrest Jan's ex-partner. They had long suspected him of drug dealing and acts of violence. To find him conscious but still stunned was a bonus, since the handcuffs slipped on so much more easily. As he left, attached to a burly constable, he swore vengeance on Jan, but this proved to be an idle threat. The police found no drugs in the house and only a small packet of amphetamines on their prisoner, so there was nothing he could do to incriminate her. A lucky escape apart from the bruises.

I returned to hospital to complete my course of radiotherapy and then another dose of cis-platin treatment, and at the end of that I was declared free of disease. Only time would tell whether I was cured. Jan and I became very close and she allowed me to share her house while I was recovering from the treatment. It seems likely that we will get married when my divorce from Stella is finalised.

One thing is clear. I will not make a balls-up of this relationship – even if I've only got one with which to do it!

CHAPTER ONE

THE INTERVIEW

Jonas had written twenty-five letters extolling his own virtues, and twenty-four universities had indicated that they were underwhelmed by his potential. So the twenty-fifth, a letter of invitation from Thames Vale University, came like a bolt from the blue.

Thames Vale was not the place he would have chosen, with its relatively poor reputation for research, but it stood on a large tree-filled campus just outside Reading, so it was probably a pleasant enough place to work. And he was getting desperate. His teaching fellowship at Brakespeare College, Oxford, was only for two years and he had no desire to work in the chemical industry. The letter from the Professor of Organic Chemistry, Horatio Courtney-Jones, explained that the department had a member of staff retiring in two years time, and that they might be able to swing some kind of deal whereby he retired early, thus releasing a new post. Coming at a time when academic posts were essentially non-existent, this was excellent news.

Jonas began to believe that his CV wasn't so bad after all. He had studied at UCL for his PhD, followed by a couple of years researching at Harvard, and now this fellowship at Oxford. He was immensely encouraged, and wrote immediately to accept the date suggested for the interview. He was bursting to tell Florence, his wife of five years, about this sudden change of luck, but she would be on the wards at the John Radcliffe Hospital, so the news would have to wait until the evening.

His afternoon was spent in combat with two tutorial groups of first-year chemistry students. He always set problems, so there was no necessity to read essays, but there was always the fear that they would not have been able to solve the problems, and then he would be forced to explain the solutions. This was a risky business, since there was always the chance that one of the more arrogant know-it-alls would disagree with his solution and become combative.

The first group seemed none too bright, despite their superlative private educations and amazing A-level results, and they listened unquestioningly to his solutions to the problems. But the second group contained two friends who had been together at Peterhouse School, and they always looked for flaws in his arguments.

"Haven't you forgotten a power of ten in that second equation?" the first one asked him. Jonas played for time while he scanned the sea of figures on the whiteboard. "No, it's included in the units for the rate of reaction," he affirmed with authority.

"Well what about the temperature of reaction – is that taken care of ?" asked the second know-it-all, a persistent thorn in the side whose exam marks always revealed a high degree of ignorance. Jonas knew this was deliberate interference.

"I think if you look carefully you'll see the temperature term is in line three," Jonas told him with a hint of a sneer.

"I still don't get it," the first student admitted. "Can you go through it all again?"

Jonas ignored this question, since he knew it was merely a delaying tactic. "No, I would rather cover the other questions" he replied. "I suggest you look up the answer in your lecture notes." He added under his breath: "which you haven't got because you didn't go to the lectures". Jonas didn't blame him, because Dobson was a useless bloody lecturer, but it still wasn't his problem. He was just a humble teaching fellow.

The tutorial dragged on for a further 40 minutes, with occasional sniping from their side and a dogged resistance from Jonas. He felt drained after they had filed out of his room – well not actually his room, since he shared it with the Fellow of Ancient English, a man who had been a friend of J R R Tolkien. Like most of the Fellows at Brakespeare he was a charming but ineffectual soul, more at home absorbed within the text of Beowulf than in any aspect of normal life. Jonas always tried to make conversation whenever they met, but it was near impossible to maintain eye contact, let alone rational intercourse, and the Fellow usually exited at the earliest opportunity.

Jonas left college as soon as he had tidied away all traces of the tutorial, and cycled home up the Cowley Road and onwards to the village of Horspath, just the other side of the ring road. He and Florence were living in a rented bungalow halfway up the steep hill that ran through the village.

Florence had had a reasonable day on the wards. The ward sister had been on leave for the day, so as staff nurse, Florence had more to do than usual. She was working on a female elderly care ward, and much of the day had been taken up ensuring that the patients were fed, washed and comfortable and getting as many of them out of bed as possible. Fortunately no one had died and the only disturbance to the daily routine had been a surprise visit by Matron. She had processed from bed to bed rather like a general inspecting the troops, making polite conversation where it was possible, and mostly receiving very little response.

There had been one minor upset when she had stopped at the bed of a confused ninety-year-old diabetic from one of the poorer parts of Oxford, who when asked how she was feeling told her to fuck off. Matron had taken this in her stride, merely glancing at Florence, who was fighting to contain a giggle.

Florence heard Jonas wheel his bike along the side-path of their bungalow. She was peeling potatoes at the sink with her back to the kitchen door. If he had had a good day, she knew he would creep up behind her, throw his arms around her, then nuzzle her neck. She rather liked this and was not disappointed this time.

"Great news – I've got a job interview at Thames Vale University" he said. She turned and gave him a peck on the cheek. "Hey, well done. When's the interview?"

"Next week, March 6th. I'm really chuffed." He gave her a big hug. "I don't suppose there's time for a quick one before dinner?"

She pushed him away and laughed. "No there isn't. And anyway I thought we'd agreed to hold off until I ovulate."

After five years of marriage they had decided to start a family. Since the books claimed that abstinence for a week prior to ovulation could be helpful, they had decided to give it a try. Florence always reckoned she could feel herself ovulate, and was keeping Jonas under restraint. "When you come back from your interview next week it should be just right, you can have your wicked way with me then – but not before!"

On the day of the interview, Jonas decided to take their car – an orange VW Beetle – rather than the train. Florence had been to town and bought him a new tie, a psychedelic mix of patterns and colours which she had seen on a mannequin in the window of Take 6. Unable to find one in the shop, she had removed the one in the window display. This, together with a new white shirt from M&S and his relatively unused dark blue suit, ensured that he looked presentable.

"You look quite handsome in a suit and tie," she told him as he paraded for her inspection. "You should dress up more often."

"Not very practical when you work in the lab or write on

a whiteboard with coloured pens all day, but thank you for the compliment" he replied.

Florence had the day off, and he dropped her at the bus stop near the top of the Cowley Road so she could travel into Oxford to meet a friend for shopping and gossip. She kissed him on the cheek as she got out of the car.

"Best of luck, and don't forget to hurry home" she said. He watched her trotting towards the bus stop, sexy in her tight black skirt and floral blouse, quite skinny with pert little breasts and lovely legs.

It was a glorious spring morning, and he enjoyed the drive towards Reading via Wallingford and along the Thames through Pangbourne. The university campus was just outside the main sprawl of Reading on the A4, and he had no trouble finding it. He was directed to a car park by the main administration building and then to a waiting room on the fourth floor of the building. His palms were sweating profusely and he had a serious case of butterflies, but he was soon put out of his misery of anticipation, and ushered into the interview room.

The four members of the interview panel were arranged around three sides of a long oblong table, with the chairman at the far end. Jonas took his place at the other end facing the chairman, who then introduced the panel.

"W-w-welcome to Thames Vale, Dr McManus" he began. "I am Professor Cyril Tilehurst and I am Dean of this F-f-f-faculty and also P-p-p-professor of Zoology. L-l-let me introduce mmm-my colleagues."

Jonas found the stammer and the slight facial tic that accompanied it off-putting to start with, but it somehow seemed in character with the elderly, white-haired professor who faced him.

"This is Professor Duncan Burnside, he's Professor of Physical Chemistry" continued Professor Tilehurst. He indicated the thin, almost bald man to his left, who had that intense look of someone who believes that they are very important. Burnside nodded. "And this is Professor David Tweetie, Professor of Inorganic Chemistry." The rather plump, middle-aged man to the right of the chairman nodded. Jonas noted that he too had a tic which involved a tightening of the facial muscles and then a leftward flick of the head. What sort of pressures must these guys be under to give them all this facial movement, Jonas wondered.

"And last but certainly not least - Professor Courtney-Jones, Professor of Organic Chemistry, who I believe wrote to you inviting you to this interview."

Courtney-Jones smiled beatifically. He was the most friendly-looking member of the bunch, though he had a piercing gaze that suggested an intensity of feeling. He was the only member of the panel Jonas knew anything about. His main claim to fame was his work on the oxidation of polycyclic aromatic hydrocarbons and the reactions of their oxidised products with DNA. This was believed to be a primary cause of certain cancers. More controversially, he had recently written a series of newspaper articles condemning the use of tetraethyl lead as an additive in petrol. This had caused major discomfort for the oil companies.

"Right – I think you should start, Professor Burnside," suggested Professor Tilehurst. Burnside pulled himself upright in his chair, fixed Jonas with a self-important stare and began his questioning.

"Can I begin by asking you whether you believe mathematics 'A' level should be a requirement for the study of chemistry at university?"

Jonas thought this was an obvious trick question from a physical chemist. Answer yes and he would have to give examples of its importance in organic chemistry. Say no and he would have to explain how the students would cope with all the equations in physical chemistry. He tried to take a middle line.

"My own view is that it is desirable but not absolutely necessary, as long as you remember to teach the requisite maths as you go along."

"Can you give me an example?"

Jonas took a deep breath. "Well – I have a tutorial problem that involves looking at different rates of reaction between laboratory processes and the corresponding enzyme-mediated processes from biology. This gets the students looking at powers of ten and logarithms. If necessary I teach them the relevant maths."

Burnside seemed satisfied and moved on to his own speciality. "Supposing I have unearthed a glass artefact. Do you know how Raman spectroscopy can help to identify the authenticity of ancient glass?"

Oh bollocks! How the hell should I know, Jonas wondered.

What the heck had that to do with his suitability to be a lecturer in organic chemistry? He plucked an answer out of the air.

"Well- I imagine you could compare its Raman spectrum with the spectra of pieces of glass of known ages until you get a match."

Amazingly that seemed to satisfy Burnside, though he seemed to have been angered that Jonas could answer the question, because he now fixed him with his most intense stare and asked: "You don't have many research publications. Why is that?"

Jonas wanted to plant a knife between his eyes. What a pompous ass!

"I have two papers from my PhD work and one in press covers some of my postdoc research – and I think this is about average for someone at my stage of career."

"A physical chemist would have many more."

Fortunately Professor Tilehurst intervened before Jonas could reach across the table and seize Burnside by the throat.

"I think w-w-w-we should m-m-move on, Professor Tweetie" he said. Tweetie's face seemed to move out of his control, with twitches and grimaces, then his head lurched to the left and he began his questioning

"Do you use metals in any of your research?"

"If you mean do I employ organometallic chemistry in my syntheses, the answer is yes. Mainly organomagnesium and organolithium reagents." That was easy.

"I'm very keen on tin myself. Use any organotin reagents?"

"So far no – and I would avoid them if I could because of their toxicity."

Tweetie's face formed itself into a leer.

"Oh, we mustn't be afraid of a bit of toxicity" he guffawed loudly. "No more questions."

Professor Tilehurst seemed a little nonplussed by Tweedie's apparent lack of interest, but he invited Professor Courtney-Jones to begin his interrogation.

"I see from your CV that you worked for Professor Elias van Esslin in the States. What did you achieve?" At last, an uncomplicated question.

"I was working on a total synthesis of prostaglandin A2. I managed to complete it by the time I left."

"That's quite an achievement. Very impressive."

Jonas assumed that Courtney-Jones was trying to convince the others that he was employable, and the second question seemed to have political undertones alerting the Dean to a lack of funds in the chemistry department.

"I'm afraid that we are seriously short of money in our department. Do you have contacts in industry who could fund your research?"

Jonas was ready for that one. "I have been in contact with Glaxo and I think they will fund a studentship for me, if I get the job."

"Good show – that's what we need, a bit of initiative." This was almost sycophantic, but Jonas was happy to convince him further of his fund-raising potential.

"I also have a good friend at Eli Lilley in Bagshot, who I think will help."

"Even better. What about teaching – would you be happy to teach the second and third year courses of my colleague who is due to retire? I do all of the first year teaching myself. Got to make sure the little blighters are brought up to scratch after the ludicrous teaching they get at school."

That was a no-brainer. "Of course – I would expect to have a substantial teaching load."

"No further questions."

Jonas felt very creepy saying that, but he knew he should support Courtney-Jones' confidence in him.

Professor Tilehurst asked him a few general questions about his present contract and when he could start. "If we offer you the p-p-position, I will leave P-professor Courtney-Jones to discuss with you the availability of l-l-l-lab space and whether he can make available a sss- small amount of money so you can b-b-b-buy some equipment and chemicals. B-b-but I doubt it will be much since they're always t-t-telling me how hard up they are!" He chuckled.

"Right – thank you Dr M-m-McManus. We will try to be in touch l-l-later today. Does Professor Courtney-Jones have your ph-ph-phone number?"

"Yes, it's on my CV."

Tilehurst gave him a beaming smile and indicated that the interview was over. Jonas breathed a sight of relief and left the room.

It was only now that he felt the wet patches under his arms and the sweat trickling down his back, but also a sense of elation that the whole thing had gone reasonably well. Now he only had to wait for the phone call.

★ ★ ★ ★ ★

He drove home in something of a daze, narrowly missing a deer which leapt from the woods into the road just outside Pangbourne. The shock brought him back to a better state of alertness, but he still couldn't remember much about the journey when he parked on their drive and got out of the car.

Florence came out to meet him. He noticed that she was wearing the short red floral dress he liked. It accentuated her curves.

"How'd it go?"

"Very well, I think. They were very kind to me with their questions – well, most of them. There were a couple of buffoons who were a bit awkward. They're going to phone me."

"Great. Come on then, I think I ovulated this afternoon."

Jonas needed no further encouragement. They grappled a bit in the hall, kissing and stroking, then advanced, without disentangling, into the main bedroom, whose curtains were already drawn. Jonas fumbled with her bra fastening while she wrenched at his trouser fly. Then they were onto the bed with underwear being shed, both seriously aroused.

Then the phone rang.

"Oh fuck, leave it!" said Jonas. But Florence, still wearing her dress, had already rolled out from under him and was heading towards the phone in the hall.

"No, it might be about your job. Hello, Florence McManus speaking?" She waved the phone at him. "It's Professor Courtney-Jones for you."

Jonas struggled from the bed wearing only his shirt, his erection deflating.

"Hello, yes. Oh thank you, that's great news. I look forward to hearing from you." He was aware of Florence standing behind him. Her hand took hold of his penis.

"Oooh – aah – I think I can start in a couple of months. Thank you again for your help. Goodbye."

He put the phone down and turned to make a grab at Florence, but she scampered back to the bed. "Come on, my egg is waiting!" Jonas needed no second invitation.

CHAPTER TWO

THE HOUSE

Florence knew she was pregnant when she threw up on the ward one morning. She made it to the sink in the sluice room just in time, but this still startled the staff nurse, who was emptying a bedpan.

"You OK?" Florence wiped her mouth.

"Well, sort of – I think I'm pregnant."

"Christ! You happy about that?"

"Yes. We'd decided to try, but I wasn't expecting it to work first time."

"Well, congrats. Roll on your maternity leave, then you can escape from this place."

But Florence knew there was a lot to do before that. They had to find a house somewhere near Reading; she had to look for a new job, and only then could she think about the baby.

On their first house-hunting trip, she visited the Thames Vale University Health Centre to register with them. The waiting room was full of students trying to look ill so they could get some time off lectures, or feigning depression to get some Valium, so Florence had to wait quite a while to see a doctor. She eventually saw a plump lady doctor called Rowlandson who examined her, and Florence was immediately glad that she had held out for a female doctor.

The internal examination was not painful, but it still seemed odd to have someone poking about inside you.

"I think you're about twelve weeks. Does that agree with your estimations?"

"Yes, I'm pretty sure when I conceived."

"Right, I'll send a letter to the Royal Berks Hospital and they will contact you. They've got a new maternity unit, it's in a charming old Victorian building." She peered over her spectacles. "Just the sort of place I'd like to have my babies – if only I could get pregnant. Probably need to lose some weight first."

She smiled at Florence. "OK, look after yourself. Make an appointment to see me in a couple of months. Also, take this form to the nurse. She'll take some blood for testing."

Florence drove to the campus near the Union. She had arranged to meet Jonas after her appointment and his first visit to the Chemistry Department. He was already waiting near the coffee bar, and they went in and ordered a couple of cappuccinos.

"How d'you get on?" he asked her, taking her hand and giving it a squeeze. "How is our little sproglet?"

"Oh fine – I didn't much like the internal examination, but otherwise it was all easy. I'm going to have it at the Royal Berks Hospital – I think we passed it on the way here. It's got a big frontage with Doric pillars and stuff."

"Oh yes, I think I know where you mean."

"They've got a new maternity unit, which sounds nice. What about your morning?"

"It went very well. I've seen my office and small lab for

research. It's all a bit scruffy and ill-equipped after Oxford, but beggars can't be choosers."

Florence looked concerned. "I hope you haven't made a mistake."

"No - it'll be fine. Because it's a relatively lowly department it should be easier to make a name for myself. And Courtney-Jones is a nice guy – a bit eccentric but he seems to really want me, so he'll do all he can to help."

He fished out a crumpled newspaper from his bag. "I bought the local rag and it's got some quite interesting-looking houses advertised." Jonas turned towards the back of the paper. "I specially like the sound of this one: 'For Sale – small pond complete with frogs - house included. £12,500'."

"Sounds like a bunch of comedians. Can we afford it?"

"Probably not, but maybe my parents can give us a small loan. Anyway, I rang the owners and we can go round after lunch."

They drove out to the small Thamesside village of Sonning and had lunch at the Crown Inn, a very old pub with oak beams, low ceilings and dirty cream paint on the uneven walls, clearly the result of decades of tar-laden cigarette smoke. The food was excellent, and it seemed reasonable after Oxford prices. The sun came out just as they collected their food, so they sat in the pub garden, which overlooked the village church.

"This is rather nice. Pity we can't afford to live here," Florence sighed.

"Yes – it's probably only affordable if you're an airline pilot. Besides you'd have further to go to the shops."

"I shan't be able to go to the shops when we have the baby."

"Are you going to try for a job in Reading before your maternity leave?"

Florence looked pensive. "I'm sure I can work for an agency, though it might mean lots of night duty. I could do that for a while. Let's find out where we're going to live, then I'll start looking."

They finished their meal and then, after consulting their Reading A-Z, drove the short distance to Radford Road, where the pond with a house was located. First impressions were excellent; it was a short road with only twenty houses. They were Edwardian or 1930s, and all but two were semi-detached. The house they had come to see was number 8 and the left-hand half of an Edwardian semi. Its bright purple door was an immediately attractive feature to both of them.

Jonas applied his hand somewhat tentatively to the door knocker, but there was no response. "Here, let me give it a knock," said Florence impatiently, and attacked the knocker, making the whole door resonate. From within there came a petulant cry, a deep woman's voice.

"OK, OK - we're not deaf!" it said. The door was flung open to reveal a ruddy-faced woman, probably in her early forties, with a large frame, a huge bust and a very bohemian appearance. Her long hair was a mass of orange curls, and she wore a long, flowing gypsy skirt. Her neck was festooned with necklaces.

"You must be Mr and Mrs McManus" she beamed. "Come in." They stepped into a long corridor which seemed to run the length of the house. "I'm Polly" she said, shaking hands with both of them. "My husband works at Reading University and he's just got a new job at Warwick, so we're being forced to move. Bloody annoying actually, because we love this place."

She waved her arm in the general direction of the back of the house. "I think it's best if you just wander around. We've got a sitting room on the first floor and then three bedrooms including one in the attic. Just poke around as much as you want. The washing machine has caused a minor flood and I need to clear up the mess."

She wandered off into the kitchen, which was to the left of the corridor.

The first thing that struck both Florence and Jonas as they moved from room to room was the sheer quantity of stuff. Every shelf, tabletop, mantelpiece and work surface was covered with articles ranging from books of all kinds to jars of pencils and biros, piles of letters and postcards, ornaments, small toys, glass animals, Christmas decorations and innumerable photos, which also adorned most of the walls. Beyond this clutter you could see the original Edwardian features of the house; the plaster light mouldings, the picture rails and the architraves. In some rooms there were huge and rather hideous wooden structures – cupboards, dressers and shelf units which were obviously the products of home carpentry. But in others, like the upstairs sitting room, there was elegant furniture, such as a commodious chesterfield sofa and a French chaise longue. Every single room had a fireplace, and the back room downstairs had a wonderful mock Adam one. This room led into a somewhat broken-down loggia and thence into the small walled garden, which was a riot of colour from shrubs and spring flowers. At the end of the garden was the pond, and presumably the frogs.

Florence and Jonas barely said a word, but it was obvious to each of them that they both loved the house. The possibilities were immense, and for the money it was a bargain. They returned to find Polly in the kitchen on her hands and knees with a sponge and bowl.

"We love it" Florence told her, "I hope there's no one else interested."

Polly got up from the floor and wiped her hands down her skirt. "Well – there is another couple, about your age, but they were so rude about my Eric's carpentry and full of their plans for knocking walls down. We don't really want to sell to them."

"Great" said Florence. Jonas added at once: "We'll find a solicitor today and try to get things moving. You're not with an estate agent are you?"

"No – bunch of crooks. Charge you a fortune and do nothing for the money." She showed them to the door. "Let us know how you get on. I take it you've got the mortgage sorted?"

Jonas hastily reassured her that this was the case, and they drove off in the Beetle. But of course they hadn't and that was the next stop - a trip to the local Halifax Building Society. Jonas had a savings account with the Oxford branch, but while they were in Reading it made sense to visit the local branch. They found this next to the central post office and were quickly shown into a small, windowless office which smelt of BO. The reason soon became apparent when they were joined by a rotund middle-aged man who seemed to be sweating from every pore.

"I believe you want to discuss the possibility of a mortgage," he wheezed. Jonas nodded. "Yes – we've seen a house we want to buy. It's £12,500."

"And how much do you have saved with us?"

"It's around, erm, £100."

The man's jaw gaped momentarily, but he quickly recovered, although he began to shuffle his ample bottom uncomfortably on the swivel chair.

"I have a Lectureship at the University with an annual salary of £3,300," Jonas reassured him.

The man didn't look markedly reassured, just even more sweaty. "How much deposit can you raise?" he asked.

Jonas plucked a purely imaginary figure from the air. "I'm pretty sure we can find £1,500."

There was a sharp intake of breath from Florence, but she quickly turned this into a cough and a beatific smile.

"Well, that would make a big difference. I'll give you all the necessary forms and you can make an appointment to see one of our advisors when you have completed them." He paused and gave Jonas a quizzical look. "And we would, of course, have to have the £1,500 transferred to this branch."

"Oh yes, of course."

Once outside the building, Florence took Jonas' arm and poked him in the ribs.

"You've been holding out on me, Mr Moneybags. Where the hell are you going to get £1,500?"

"I told you – I'm hoping my parents will be able to help."

* * * * *

Stanley McManus was piling more lopped apple branches onto his bonfire, which was currently more smoke than fire. In fact he kept disappearing as tendrils of smoke wrapped themselves around him, and it was not immediately apparent that he was wearing an old school green and red rugby shirt and a pair of blue tracksuit bottoms. The elastic had long ago exceeded Young's modulus of elasticity, and they were held up with a length of string.

"Hi Dad!" Jonas called from the top of the long garden. Then, laughing, he turned to Florence and said: "That's my old rugby kit."

"No disappointment there then. The most elegantly attired father-in-law a girl could want!"

Stanley waved his garden fork at them and walked up the garden towards them. He was in his late 60s, a shambling figure with sloping shoulders and just a few strands of wispy hair. His growing 'corporation', as he called it, could be seen over the top of his track suit bottoms. He was puffing on a small cheroot.

"And how's my favourite nurse?" he asked, bending down to give Florence a peck on the cheek. "I thought that little'un might be beginning to show." He nodded towards Florence's four-month bump, which was nearly obscured by her Laura Ashley dress.

"She's built like a sparrow Dad, I don't suppose she'll get very large," added Jonas.

"Your mother was huge – could hardly get out of bed in the end."

Further discussion of Norma McManus' pregnancy was disrupted by the appearance of the lady herself, who appeared at the top of the garden telling them that dinner was ready. Norma was also in her sixties, four years younger than Stanley, a former Dartford Harrier who looked far too small and rounded to have ever run competitively. She was one of those happy-go-lucky people who never have a harsh or critical word about anybody, though you would not necessarily want her on your team in a game of Scrabble. Like Stanley, she had left school at 15, but unlike him she had never been much good at English or Maths and had somehow muddled through by learning shorthand and typing. They were both now retired but had worked all their lives in clerical posts for a local refrigeration company. It was unsurprising that they were very proud of Jonas' educational achievements and were also delighted with his choice of wife; they thought Florence was wonderful, especially now that she was carrying their first grandchild.

Sunday lunch was always a treat, albeit a predictable one. It consisted of overcooked slices of roast beef partially rehydrated with black Bisto gravy, four different vegetables and roast potatoes, followed by either strawberry crumble or

Bakewell tart, both benefiting hugely from the butter dish and the latter containing enough jam and ground almonds for at least four tarts. What the gravy did for the beef, a large jug of thick yellow custard did for the desserts. Stanley loved his custard and jealously guarded the jug.

Florence ate like a bird as usual and attracted comment from Stanley. "You're not eating enough to keep yourself alive, let alone that baby" he chided. But Norma sprang to her defence. "Oh do be quiet Stanley!" she snapped. "She's got a small frame, not great big bones and a corporation like you."

"But I was going to have seconds of crumble" Florence reassured him, "and I have put on nearly five pounds already."

"Yes, she's got a nice little bump under that dress," Jonas said, adding his support.

"Well I still think she eats like a wren," Stanley grunted.

Norma rose from the table. "Come on Florence, let's go and talk babies over the washing up" she said. Florence winked at Jonas. This was his chance to raise the topic of the loan. Stanley helped himself to a further generous portion of strawberry crumble and custard.

"Dad" began Jonas, "Florence and I have found a superb house in Reading that we'd like to buy. The problem is, we can't get a mortgage unless we can find £1,500 for a deposit."

Stanley lowered the full spoonful of crumble that was about to enter his mouth. He looked a bit surprised. "I'm not sure we have that kind of money" he said. "Or rather we probably do, but I don't know whether we can spare it. Can Florence's parents help?"

"Not at the moment. They are saving up to pay for Florence's sister's wedding – she's having something rather exotic."

Stanley chewed thoughtfully on a mouthful of dessert. "OK, I'll ask your mother. She'll probably say it's OK." He finished up the last dregs of custard from the jug, then went to find Norma. Jonas thought his 'corporation' had enlarged even since lunch began.

It only took a few minutes for the answer to come. Norma emerged from the kitchen, removing her yellow Marigolds as she came.

"Of course we can find the money" she smiled. "After all we will need somewhere to stay when we come to see our grandchildren."

Jonas gave her a big hug. "Thanks Mum, but we're only having one to start with."

"Yes, but there'll be lots more. Florence has been telling me she wants at least four." That was the moment Jonas knew that he and Florence would always be poor.

CHAPTER THREE

THE MOVE

A white Ford Transit sat on the drive, surrounded by Jonas and Florence's worldly possessions. Since the bungalow was furnished, they had only a few items of their own furniture: a coffee table; a red rocking chair (a wedding present from Florence's favourite grandmother); a newly-acquired brass bed (claimed to be haunted by the junkshop owner, who had been glad to be rid of it for £25); chemistry books, paperback novels, LPs and a twelve-inch black-and-white TV. What they lacked in furniture they made up for with boxes of dresses and skirts and blouses from Biba and Laura Ashley, not all in fashion but too good to throw away, bundles of faded *Eagle* comics, assorted kitchenware, mostly from Habitat, a small quantity of richly-patterned American bed linen and towels and two boxes of mementos from their time in the USA. These last boxes contained, among other things, a beaten tin candlestick holder from somewhere in Maine; a strange-looking multi-coloured ceramic bird from Baja California; a red wooden Pilgrim father-type statuette marked with an H for Harvard; and an orange coffee set whose cups were too small to provide more than the merest shot of caffeine. All of this would later end up at a car boot sale, but it provided a moment of nostalgia for Jonas as he loaded the van while

Florence cleaned the bungalow. She knew her efforts would not be enough, since the landlady, a retired woman from Maidenhead, had on previous inspection visits found reason to complain about talc on the bathroom floor, porridge in the sink drainer and cobwebs on the lampshades, amongst other gripes. But she was determined to do her best to leave the place in as clean a state as possible.

Florence's bump was now beginning to show, and she was finding work at the Radcliffe more tiring. She was going to work for two more months, commuting by train from Reading three days a week, and would then take her maternity leave from the beginning of October.

By late morning they were both finished with their labours. After a brief break for coffee and digestives, they locked up and drove into Oxford to return the keys to the estate agent who looked after the property.

"Did you sort out the garden before you left?" he asked them. This was a bone of contention, since the owner had provided only a hand mower with blunt blades and a rusty fork and spade. Neither Jonas or Florence had any interest in gardening, but both had made an effort to keep the garden free of weeds and the lawn mown.

"Well, we've done our best with the rubbish equipment we were given, but I'm sure she'll have the professionals in and then charge us for their efforts," Jonas told him cynically. The estate agent nodded sagely. "I'll do my best for you, but it was part of the contract that you would look after her garden."

They knew there was no point arguing. Their security

deposit would be whittled away by disbursements for unnecessary cleaning and gardening, but that was the price you paid for living in rented accommodation.

They left Oxford in a state of annoyance and frustration, made worse by the fact that a letter had arrived just that morning from the Oxford University Chest. This informed Jonas that he was in breach of contract for leaving his Fellowship at Brakespeare College after one year rather than two. This would necessitate repayment of half the travel grant he had received to help with their passage from the USA to Oxford. While annoying, this was not actually unreasonable, and Jonas had already resolved to ask if he could repay the £650 in monthly instalments over the next year.

To cheer themselves up, they stopped once again at the Crown in Sonning for a pub lunch in the garden. After the meal and a pint each, they felt ready to collect the keys for 8 Radford Road from their solicitor, Mr Snelgrove. His office was on London Street, a road leading away from the centre of Reading. It was full of what purported to be antique emporia but were in fact little more than slightly up-market junk shops.

"We'll have to have in look in these places once we move in," said Florence enthusiastically. Jonas merely grunted. He knew their finances would not allow for frivolous purchases.

"Oh look, I like those chairs," announced Florence. Jonas took her hand and dragged her in through the door of Mr Snelgrove's modest practice. Mr Snelgrove heaved himself out of his chair as they were shown in. An ample beer belly hung over the top of an imitation snakeskin belt, and a plaid tie with one very long end sticking out from a mostly unbuttoned beige M&S cardigan added to a generally crumpled appearance.

"Have a seat will you, and I'll just go through the paperwork." he said. He slumped back into his plush leather swivel chair as they sat uncomfortably on the cheap plastic chairs provided. "Everything seems to be in order" he said. "The building society has said that they want you to fix the roof – it's uneven – and their surveyor also found evidence of woodworm in the loft. All to be expected in a 1909 house, so I shouldn't worry too much. The previous owners have left you some curtain rails and a fitted stair carpet, but not much else I am afraid. Any questions?"

"What's the timescale for fixing the roof etc?" enquired Jonas, conscious of the financial constraints they were under.

The solicitor smiled. "Oh, I shouldn't rush to do anything. They always find something to complain about, but they never seem to check if anything has been done about it. I would ignore it."

He paused to see if there was anything else they wanted to know, but it was clear to Jonas and Florence that they were wasting his valuable time, so they just nodded their assent.

"Right, I'll get my secretary to dig out the keys and you can move in to your new home" said Mr Snelgrove. "I hope you'll be very happy. You'll receive our final account in a few days." He again heaved himself to his feet and shook their hands.

Once outside, keys in hand, Jonas headed quickly for the van, but the call he was fearing intercepted him before he could reach it.

"Couldn't we just have a peep at those chairs Jonas?" she asked him. He shrugged, turned around and joined her at the entrance to the antique shop. The four chairs were on the pavement, and he had to agree that they looked solid enough, and they appeared to be woodworm free.

"They're late Victorian," the shop-owner informed them, having appeared suddenly through the shop door, no doubt anxious for a sale in troubled times. "Notice the elegantly curved legs and claw feet. I can take ten per cent off the price if you're paying cash."

"What is the price?" asked Jonas.

"£60 for the four chairs – a real bargain." Florence looked pleadingly at Jonas.

"Make it £50 and we'll take them."

"£55 and they're yours."

"£52 – and that's my last offer."

The owner looked hurt, but he held out his hand to Jonas. "You're a hard man. How am I to make a living?"

"And how am I to support a wife and child?" Jonas handed over the cash and the two men carried the chairs to the Transit. Florence had a beaming smile on her face. Once inside the van, she gave Jonas a kiss on the cheek.

"I'm hoping for a bigger reward than that!" Jonas suggested. "Once we get the haunted bed assembled."

"You're such a lecherous devil! All you ever think about."

But secretly she was very happy; she had never expected to get the chairs. She knew money was very tight, but they did need something to sit on apart from the red rocking chair.

Jonas drove the short distance to Radford Road, where they were able to park right outside their new house. The dustbin was overflowing onto the small front garden. Several full boxes stood alongside, obviously the products of a last-minute clearance. Inside there was a faint smell of mould, mingling with a kind of empty dustiness. Florence sneezed.

"They obviously didn't have time to clean much," she observed.

"But they did have time to remove the light bulbs" Jonas commented as he tried a couple of the light switches. They had, in fact, left just one bulb downstairs and one upstairs.

"And this stair carpet has seen better days," Florence remarked as she pointed to the almost threadbare carpet. "Let's hope the curtain rails are in better nick." They were – all two of them – though this was somewhat academic, since they didn't have any curtains.

They slowly unpacked the van, Jonas trying to carry in all the heaviest items, leaving Florence to unload the numerous carrier bags full of books and mementos. After half an hour the front room was full of their worldly possessions: suitcases, boxes, carrier bags, bits of brass bed, a coffee table, a red rocking chair, some framed prints, a record player, a TV and the four Victorian chairs.

"Not much to show for five years of wedded bliss," sighed Florence. "But I'm sure the house will soon be full of new things – not to mention a baby." He stroked her bump. "Come on, let's get the bed erected."

"You erect it – I'm going to get my kitchen stuff unpacked."

Jonas set about carrying the brass bed components up the stairs and into the front bedroom, which was the largest of the three. The two side bars slotted easily into the large brass ends and the heavy baseboard rested neatly on top. Finally he heaved the mattress up the stairs – no mean feat – and dragged it onto the base board. Then the moment of truth as he collapsed onto the bed. It was immediately obvious that they needed a new mattress, as the huge springs bored into his back. Another expense they could ill afford.

Meanwhile in the kitchen, Florence was scrubbing every surface prior to distributing her kitchenware between the numerous drawers and cupboards, obviously the products of the amateur carpentry of the previous owner. Although she knew little of tenon joints and housing joints, she recognised inferior examples in every drawer and shelf. Huge screws seemed to hold each unit firmly against the wall, promising to make Jonas' life difficult in the future whenever a unit was disassembled for the purposes of interior reorganisation and decoration.

Several bowls of black water ended up in the double drainer sinks before Florence was happy with her new kitchen. "Cup of tea Jonas?" she called up the stairs, and he was only too glad to stop his own efforts to clean their bedroom and the bathroom.

The latter boasted an original Edwardian bath and toilet, with its ornamental chain and mahogany seat. "Phew, the place is filthy," he announced. "But hey, the kitchen looks great. You've worked hard."

"How's the bed – seen the ghost yet?"

"No ghost. And we're not going to have much fun on that mattress. The springs would leave us black and blue."

"That's a relief then, you won't want sex any more." Grinning, Florence brought their mugs of tea and Jonas carried two of their new chairs out into the garden. This involved passing from the kitchen to the back room, with its mock Adam fireplace, then through a French window which led into a rather scruffy loggia, and finally onto the lawn. This had lush and very long grass that desperately needed cutting.

"We need so much stuff," sighed Jonas. "I wonder if my dad has still got his old mower."

"I bet he has. Your dad never throws anything away, he's the original Womble."

Jonas laughed. "It's bound to be tied up with gaffer tape and wire though."

They drank in silence while they looked around, weighing up the jobs that needed doing. The loggia had a shelf unit from which the paint had mostly peeled, with a disused bird's nest on the top shelf. Its one supporting wooden upright bore the unmistakeable signs of rot at its base, and the plastic gutter was hanging loose at one point. At the end of the garden an old wooden shed seemed to be more or less intact, though the door hung open on one hinge.

"Why didn't we see all these things when we looked around?" asked Jonas. "The shed, the loggia, a garden full of old shrubs and weeds." But he knew the answer to his own question. They had fallen in love with the house; its imperfections had seemed unimportant.

Florence squeezed his hand: "Never mind" she said. "We've got loads of time to fix it, and it'll be fun doing up our very own house."

"Absolutely. Anyway, back to the coalface. Can't sit around chatting to you all day."

Florence made a start on the front room while Jonas used an old home-made wooden ladder he had found in the shed to climb up into the loft. It was black with the filth that had entered through the roof. This, he now realised, was simply tiles on battens with no roofing felt, the way they used to do roofs in 1909. A large galvanised water tank held pride of place to the right of the loft trapdoor, with a muddle of water pipes entering and leaving the tank. In one corner there was a bent and broken doll's pram which was probably big enough for a real baby. An orange trunk had also been abandoned, its lid gaping open.

Jonas heaved himself up into the loft and peered into the trunk. It contained some yellowing newspapers and a motorcycle helmet, but nothing else. At least the roof looked sound and the loft had been partially boarded at floor level. Jonas thought it was crying out to be converted into a fourth bedroom - when they had some spare money.

He clambered back down the ladder, bringing with him piles of black dust. That reminded him of another thing they needed – a vacuum cleaner. He collected their dustpan and brush and relieved Florence of her bumper box of Flash, then began to clean the bathroom. Florence was opening up all the many homemade cupboards in the front room and the adjacent dining room.

Apart from several large spiders and some smaller six-legged creatures, the previous owners had bequeathed them very little. One drawer contained a pack of assorted food dyes with a printed pre-decimal price of one shilling and seven pence. She assumed this meant that the constituent chemicals would be nasty ones, so put it on one side to await a decision from Jonas. The only other discovery was three old jumpers stuffed up the front room chimney, presumably to keep out winter drafts. Florence made a mental note to remove them before they had their first fire.

Now for the cleaning.. She fetched a bowl of water, then realised that Jonas had pinched her Flash, so she had to retrieve this before she could begin to wash the bare floorboards. Jonas was hard at work scrubbing the old enamel bath, and she was pleasantly surprised to discover that he had already made a fair stab at cleaning the toilet.

"That's quite a good job you've done on the toilet – at least for a bloke!"

"Thank you kindly. My toilet training has progressed far beyond mere lid closing and drip elimination!"

She laughed: "But your training is still in its preliminary stages in many other areas" she reminded him. She took the Flash and returned downstairs.

They both worked hard until five o'clock, when Florence remembered that they didn't have any food in the house, so they set off on foot to find the local shops before they closed for the day. Radford Road was a side road off the main A329 between Reading and Wokingham, and just across this two-lane road was a large coaching inn, the Bell and Whistle, and a small parade of shops. The first, they discovered, was a surprisingly good food store called Giuseppe's, with an excellent delicatessen, accompanied by a ladies' hairdresser, a Chinese fish and chip shop and finally an old-fashioned ironmongers that boasted 'all the screws and nuts you could ever want'. "Sounds like a cross between a funny farm and a brothel," observed Jonas.

But the deli was the real find, and they were served by Giuseppe himself, a large, jovial Italian whose girth suggested that he enjoyed his own products. They bought buffalo mozzarella, some Parma ham, yeast and Italian flour for making pizza dough, together with tomatoes, butter, eggs, bread, red wine and other staples.

"Wow, what a find!" enthused Florence as they left the shop with their purchases. Florence made the pizza dough while Jonas finished off cleaning their bedroom and the bathroom. Then they sat on the new chairs to eat their slices of pizza from plates held on their laps. Since there were no curtains, they were continually aware of people peering in as they passed by.

"It's a bit like being in a goldfish bowl, "suggested Jonas. "But hey, who cares, it's our goldfish bowl. Cheers!" And they clinked their tumblers of Italian red wine, both feeling a warm glow of satisfaction with the house and their labours that afternoon.

Neither of them felt much like more cleaning after the pizza and several glasses of wine, so they wandered around the house trying to decide what to do with the various rooms – colour schemes, furniture needed, shelves to be erected. Once it got dark, as there were only two light bulbs, they went to bed.

"I see what you mean about the mattress springs," said Florence as she bounced onto the bed. "I'm up early in the morning so I hope the ghost leaves us alone on our first night."

"Should we pretend we're on the first night of our honeymoon?" suggested Jonas, knowing full well what the answer would be.

"No we shouldn't! Keep your cold hands and feet to yourself, and remember that you promised to run me to the station in the morning, so you've got an early start too."

★ ★ ★ ★ ★

They had both set their alarm clocks, but they were not needed. The absence of curtains allowed the morning light to begin streaming into the room at five o'clock, leaving them with little chance of further sleep. Florence snuggled up to Jonas and they dozed for a short while. With her train to catch at 7.15, Florence went for her bath around six while Jonas made some tea and toast.

"I hope you're going to do this every morning" Florence observed, sitting on the edge of the bed in her dressing gown sipping her tea and munching a piece of toast.

"It's all part of my training. How's the toast?"

"A bit burnt at the edges but it'll do. Nice cup of tea though."

She wiggled about on the bed, making it rattle. "We do desperately need a new mattress. I'm feeling a bit bruised this morning after a night on the springs."

"Well, let's see what my first pay cheque looks like. It ought to be better then the one I got at Oxford." Jonas reached over and kissed her on the neck. "And if it's not enough you'll have to go back to selling your body."

"Not sure anyone would want to pay for it in its present state" she replied. Jonas gave her another kiss and tried to reach round to find her breasts under the dressing gown.

"Oh, I don't know – it's not too bad" he grinned.

Florence pulled away and rose quickly from the bed to get out of his reach. "No time for that! I've got a job to go to, even if you academics can stay in bed all day." She began putting on her make-up. Jonas took the hint and went for his shave and a bath. They were both ready by 6.30 and had time for some cereal before Jonas drove her to the station.

The one-way network in Reading proved confusing, a kind of distribution system for spreading the jams more widely, but the station was well signposted, so there was no real problem. He left her in the forecourt, then returned home to have a proper breakfast and to gather books and papers for his first day at work.

The drive along the A4 towards Maidenhead was actually quite scenic, passing a small winery, a shire horse centre and several very old coaching inns. A few miles past the turn-off to Henley, a large purple sign announced the main entrance to Thames Vale University. Jonas turned in and followed the signs to the Chemistry Department. This was in a three storey building at the far end of the campus and was of a peculiar construction that could best be described as flint in concrete, a building material that it shared with many of the local churches. Unlike the churches, this product of sixties construction had not aged well, and the large window frames were already beginning to rot. The forest of chimneys on the roof, which carried the effluent from the many fume cupboards below, gave the building the appearance of a factory rather than a place of learning. Its one saving grace was a large, double helical staircase at the right-hand end of the L-shaped building. It had been designed, it was claimed, so that students arriving for lectures would ascend via the clockwise helix, while students leaving the lectures would take the anti-clockwise one. This triumph of imagination and planning never actually worked in practice, though all those who saw the staircase marvelled at the feat of engineering behind it.

The departmental 'beadle', a thin man with huge sideburns, sat in a box-like construction at the foot of the staircase. He directed Jonas to Professor Courtney-Jones' office on the second floor.

In the outer office he met Samantha.

Samantha had left school at sixteen to attend a College of Further Education. It was not that she was non-academic; she simply could not stand the regimentation at her single-sex grammar school any more. She especially detested the rigorous dress code of grey pleated skirt and green blazer, plain bras under the regulation white blouse, and certainly no duffel coats or chisel-toed shoes. The rules allowed no fraternising with the boys from the local boys' grammar at the bus stop and no eating (or smoking – God forbid!) in public. Her father had told her she was wasting her talents, but she took to shorthand and typing with great ease and even won the first-year prize for typing. The boys all wanted to go out with her, but she thought of them as her mates – good for a laugh and perhaps a kiss or two, but nothing else. Needless to say the boys thought she was a cock-tease and tried even harder to win her favours, but this just made her more determined to keep them at arm's length.

At the end of two years she was ready for a job, and after a couple of failed attempts, which she put down to being too flippant with her answers, she landed the job in the Chemistry Department. Samantha immediately hit it off with Courtney-Jones, who she described as a 'sweetie', and he returned the compliment by keeping her supplied with roses from his garden and home-made wine during the winter months. He also gave her very little to do, apart from typing letters to oil companies and the national press which he composed on his Dictaphone.

Courtney Jones was a supreme nuisance to these international oil giants, as he was fighting to get them to remove the lead from petrol. Samantha loved this part of the job, because it allowed her creative energies unlimited freedom; she took his words and turned them into prose that was both more erudite and also more penetrating. The newspapers loved the letters and always printed them, while the oil companies hated them and detested Courtney-Jones. It was so much easier for them to continue adding tetraethyl lead to petrol in order to improve its efficiency than it was to research for safer alternatives. They knew it was toxic, but they also knew that the public were only interested in getting more miles per gallon. So what the hell if it retarded learning in children, as Courtney-Jones claimed? And anyway he couldn't prove it. If they had known that they had to contend with Courtney-Jones and Samantha, they might have been more worried.

"Dr McManus – we've been expecting you," Samantha rose to her feet, swept her long mane of blonde hair off her shoulders and greeted him with a cheery grin. Jonas could not fail to notice that the hair had been obscuring a substantial bosom.

"I'm Samantha" she said. "I will be very happy to look after your needs – correspondence, copying lecture materials, chasing up tutorial non-attenders, etc."

Jonas felt very much at home; this was better than he had expected. "That's great, I hope I don't have to ask for too much help" he said.

"Oh but you must, that's what I'm here for. All the other Organic staff take advantage of me, if you see what I mean." She grinned again. "I'm afraid Professor Courtney-Jones isn't in yet, he always feeds the chickens before he comes to work. So let me show you your lab-office."

Room 230 was small, with a desk on one side, a fume cupboard just inside the door in the left-hand corner attached to a long teak bench on that side of the room, and a cupboard in the far right-hand corner. Some chemicals and glassware which Jonas had requested sat on the bench, still in their boxes.

"You've used up most of the budget for this quarter," Samantha announced, indicating the boxes with a sweep of her hand.. "Your Organic Chemistry colleagues are very cross." She giggled. "Especially Dr Grimwold. He was hoping to buy a new pressure apparatus."

"Oh dear, I didn't want to cause anyone a problem."

"Nonsense, they're just behaving like spoilt children. Jealous of the new young whiz kid from Oxford."

"Oh God, I hope they don't really think that!"

"And what if they do? It'll shake them all out of their lethargy. Now you settle in and I'll come and collect you when Professor Courtney-Jones arrives." She swept out of the room, leaving a trail of the very pleasant floral perfume which Jonas had been enjoying. There was a pleasant hint of the flirtatious about her to add to her general extroversion.

Jonas began to unpack the box of papers and books which he had brought with him from the car. There were many others to come in due course, but for now he had just brought some files pertaining to his proposed research projects and some key reference books. They looked good on the shelves over his desk, and he felt a surge of excitement about his new job. For the first time in his career he was his own boss - well, at least up to a point.

"Hello, you must be Jonas McManus" said a voice. A ruddy-faced man with a Scots accent was at the office door. He had a cheeky smile and wispy grey hair suffused with yellow streaks, probably the last remnants of red hair.

"I'm Rob Lewis, your next door neighbour" he said. He offered his right hand as Jonas rose from his chair. They shook hands and Jonas thought he could detect alcohol on his breath.

"Everyone's very nervous about your arrival," Rob announced. "Apart from me, that is. I just teach and don't do much research, so you'll not be a threat to me!" He laughed.

"I hope I won't be a threat to anyone."

"Oh they're just being paranoid. They're anxious about someone who has spent time in the States and Oxford, whilst they've never been out of Britain. They'll get over it."

"Well I hope so. I'm sure they've got lots more research papers than I have."

Rob turned to leave. "Well, if there's anything you need, just give us a shout" he finished.

As he left the office Samantha appeared beside him.

"Dr Lewis, I hope you haven't been wasting Dr McManus' time with your tales of Scottish drunkenness and lewd behaviour, or worse, quoting bits of Robbie Burns at him."

"Nothing of the kind, you brazen hussy, and I'll not hear a bad word about our greatest statesman."

"Greatest fornicator, more like!"

"There's nicht wrong wi' fornication, as I'm sure any normal pairson would agree!"

"Dr Lewis! I shall have to have words with Professor Courtney-Jones."

"He'll not listen unless you can link fornication to lead!" Lewis guffawed as he returned to his office next door. Samantha turned to speak to Jonas, seeing his puzzled expression.

"Don't take any notice of him" she said. "Dr Lewis and I like to share a little dirty chat most days, all perfectly harmless. He's really a very nice man."

"He certainly seems to be very friendly."

"The girls in his tutorial groups all love him. They treat him as a benevolent old uncle. Now, Professor Courtney-Jones has just come in, I expect he'll see you now."

She led him back to her office and knocked on the door to the inner, professorial office. The door burst open to reveal a somewhat dishevelled Courtney-Jones, presumably straight from the hen house, Jonas mused. He fixed Jonas with a firm stare, his steel grey eyes unusually intense and disconcerting.

"Ah, Dr McManus, so good to see you. Come on in and sit down. Would you like tea? Samantha can do you an Earl Grey or a PG tips."

"A cup of Earl Grey would be great."

"Right, two of those please Samantha."

He waved Jonas into an armchair beneath a set of shelves groaning with books. "How did you find the office? Ordered you as much glassware and chemicals as I thought the budget would stand. Damn inorganic chemists spend huge amounts on expensive catalysts."

Jonas opened his mouth to thank him for the supplies, but Courtney-Jones was going off at a tangent. "Let me show you these latest figures, just got them this morning, very exciting." He pulled a set of papers from his battered briefcase, then pointed to a series of tables. "Look at these blood-lead values for two local primary schools, one near the A4 and the other in the country. Huge difference!" Jonas nodded in agreement. "Now look at the two respective IQ values. Consistently lower for the school near the A4. A direct correlation with the elevated blood-lead values." His eyes burned even more brightly from under his wild, bushy eyebrows. "The oil companies cannot refute this evidence. I've finally got them on the run!"

"It does look very convincing," agreed Jonas. Then, wanting to push the conversation in the direction of his own personal needs, he asked about his duties. "What do you have in mind for me to give lectures on?"

"Oh, anything you like. As you know, I teach the first year courses, but after that you can share the rest with the other three Organic staff. Have a word with Albert Greenough, he organises the teaching roster, have you met him yet?"

"No, but I was going to seek him out after our meeting."

Further discussion was interrupted by a knock on the door and the appearance of Samantha. "Sorry to disturb you Professor Courtney-Jones, but I've got Brian Thatcher outside and he's very distressed about his mass spectrometer." She showed in a tall man with a slender yet athletic build who was red in the face and clearly unhappy. Later Jonas learned that

Thatcher was the technician in charge of the mass spectrometer and provided one of the main analytical services for the department.

"Sorry to disturb you Prof, but someone's taken the bloody helium cylinder from the mass spectrometer" he said.

"That's absurd!" roared Courtney-Jones. "It can't just have disappeared."

"Oh yes it has. It was there when I left on Friday, but it's not there this morning. Just dangling copper pipes where the cylinder was connected to the mass spec."

"Right, let's get to the bottom of this," said Courtney-Jones. He stormed out of his office with Brian Thatcher in hot pursuit. Jonas followed them at a distance, exchanging a wry smile with Samantha as he passed. Courtney-Jones had already reached the far end of the corridor, where it met, at right angles, another corridor coming from the teaching block and the main staircase. As he turned the corner, he came face to face with a small man with a thick mane of grey hair who was wheeling a large brown gas cylinder on a trolley.

"What on earth are you doing with that helium cylinder?" he blustered

"We needed it to blow up the balloons at the Rushmore End fete on Saturday" said the man. "Surely you remember? You bought a couple for your grandchildren."

Courtney-Jones' jaw dropped, while Brian Thatcher's face seemed to grow even redder. The small man continued to wheel the trolley down the corridor towards the mass spectrometer room at the end. As he passed Jonas he said cheerily: "I guess you're Jonas McManus, good to see you. I'm Noel Grimwold. Come and have a chat some time."

"It's not good enough Prof" moaned Thatcher, watching Grimwold's retreating back. "He's always taking liberties with equipment. The technicians are always complaining about him."

"I'll have a word with him, Brian" Courtney-Jones assured him. "That's another of your colleagues" he said to Jonas. "Bit of a maverick, I am afraid." With that he swept back to his office, Brian Thatcher at his heel.

Jonas was undecided as to what to do, since his meeting with Courtney-Jones had been interrupted. He thought he might as well seek out his third and final colleague, Albert Greenough, so he wandered along the corridor until he found the office which carried Greenough's name. He knocked on the door. A cheery voice invited him to enter.

"Hello, I'm Jonas McManus, I'm in the process of moving in" he said. Albert was a stocky Northerner with a beaming smile and a firm handshake.

"Hey, great to meet you, we've all been wondering when you would arrive" he said. "Take a seat."

Jonas sat down in the seat alongside Albert's desk. His office was also a lab-office, but a little larger than the one Jonas had been awarded. "Have you met the others?"

"Yes, Rob Lewis knocked on my door and I've just met Noel Grimwold, he was returning a helium cylinder he'd borrowed for Rushmore End fete. The Prof was none too pleased."

Albert laughed. "That's typical, he's always liberating stuff from the lab. Last year he got caught taking a load of cyanide home to stem an invasion of rats. He got into real trouble over that, but he takes it all in his stride. Criticism and complaints just pass him by."

Jonas moved the conversation onto business. "Professor Courtney-Jones said you would tell me what courses you want me to take."

"We assumed you would want to teach some Synthesis and Natural Products, but apart from that we all muck in and give the tutorials. We don't have that many students, so it's not very arduous." He waited for Jonas to comment.

"That's fine, if you let me have a copy of the current syllabus, I'll fit something in around it."

Albert rummaged around in his filing cabinet and handed Jonas some papers. "That should help you, not very comprehensive I'm afraid, but we've never had anyone of your calibre here before."

Jonas thought he detected just a whiff of sarcasm. Perhaps they were all a bit nervous about his arrival. He put the thought out of his mind and rose to leave.

"Thanks for that, I'll go and make a start on my lectures. This is all a bit new to me, I've only ever given tutorials before."

"Don't worry too much, our students are not of the highest quality, unlike the ones you've been used to." Again just a hint of bile. "Come back for a chat when you've had time to settle in."

Jonas went back to his office and worked on his lecture courses for the rest of the morning. Around 12.30 he took a stroll around the university campus, which encompassed a huge expanse of grassland, formal flower beds and magnificent old trees with a duck-filled lake at its centre. As the weather was fine and sunny, many students were sprawled on the grass eating their lunch while others sat at tables outside the refectory block. All in all he had come to a very pleasant place to work or be a student. He felt a glow of satisfaction as he drove off the campus on his way to meet Florence at Reading Station.

Florence felt tired as she fought her way through the throng of rush-hour travellers leaving Reading station. She spotted Jonas almost immediately waving from their car, which was parked on double yellow lines opposite the station entrance.

"Quick, get in, there's a warden coming," he urged as she reached the car and tumbled into the front passenger seat. He drove off immediately to join the queue of traffic heading for Reading prison, Oscar Wilde's least favourite poetic subject.

"God what an awful day," Florence complained. "Two deaths and a pre-menstrual sister! And then I caught the wrong train, the one that stopped at every station."

"Still it's not for long now," Jonas reassured her, "only a couple of months."

"And baby has been tumbling around like a circus performer. He obviously has my gymnastic abilities."

It was a tacit mutual assumption that their baby was a boy.

Florence wanted a boy and believed she had conceived at the 'boy time' of her cycle, though she had only limited faith in the pronouncements of women's magazines.

Jonas negotiated his way through the chaotic Reading traffic using a back route which he had discovered on the way to the station. Their new home seemed especially welcoming in the late afternoon sunshine, and they were soon enjoying a cup of tea in the garden.

"Two bits of good news," Jonas announced. "The Oxford University Chest have written to say they will allow me to repay my travel grant in monthly instalments over a year."

"That should help the finances, and the second?"

Jonas grinned with a look of self-satisfaction. "I think I have solved the problem with the mattress springs, at least for now."

"How?"

"Well, you remember the four candlewick bedspreads we got as wedding presents?"

"Yes, ghastly things."

"I've laid two of them over the mattress and it seems much less lumpy. Simple but effective."

"Brilliant, well done."

After finishing their tea, Jonas began work on their dinner, chicken breasts with Parma ham and mozzarella cheese, while Florence went for a bath. He had the TV on and heard the start of the six o'clock news: more threats of strike action from the miners and municipal workers, and a declaration from the Prime Minister, Edward Heath, that his government would not yield to threats.

Then Florence called from upstairs. "Come and see the baby leaping about, Jonas!"

He found her in their bedroom, naked apart from her knickers. "Look, he's all over the place."

A ripple moved across Florence's enlarged abdomen and then there were several sudden movements as the baby kicked. "Feel him kick."

Jonas laid his hand on her belly and felt the baby move.

"Active little rascal," he observed, "boy you look good, pregnancy suits you."

"You mean you like my new ripe melons."

"They are rather gorgeous," he agreed. With an alacrity that surprised him, considering her large belly and changed centre of gravity, she slipped off her knickers. "Come on then. But you'd better be right about the mattress."

CHAPTER FOUR

A NEW LIFE

Florence and Jonas were relaxing in the garden of his parents' house. Neither of them could move. He had eaten too much roast beef, along with five vegetables and followed by strawberry crumble, while she was trying to find somewhere to rest her heavy abdomen. Their baby was five days overdue, and her growing impatience was now overshadowing her anxiety about the whole process of childbirth.

They had attended a couple of pre-natal classes, but she knew nothing could prepare her for the actual event. At her most recent appointment, the doctor had assured her that the baby was the right way up and probably due any time. That had been a week ago, and the waiting was beginning to get on her nerves, so it was with a mixture of excitement and apprehension that she felt the first twinge of discomfort.

"Ouch, that hurt" she said, gabbing Jonas' arm. "D'you think I'm starting?"

"Christ I don't know, what was it like?"

"Like a period pain, but in a different place."

"We'd better head for home anyway."

They quickly threw their bags, including Florence's hospital bag, into the car and drove off, leaving behind a very excited set of parents who were relishing the prospect of being grandparents for the first time. Jonas drove with uncharacteristic speed and daring across London, surprising several motorists with his sudden lane changes, especially at Hyde Park Corner and the Hammersmith flyover. Soon they were speeding towards Reading along the M4, and Florence was indicating that the pains were getting more frequent.

"How frequent?" Jonas enquired.

"About every ten minutes."

"That doesn't seem very frequent."

"All right for you to say that, you're not having them!"

She feigned silent annoyance for a while, until a particularly painful twinge caused her to cry out. "Ouch, bloody hell! Can't you go any faster?"

Jonas put his foot down and they hurtled even more recklessly towards the Royal Berkshire Hospital. The maternity unit was at the back of the main building and was, so they had been told, due for replacement, but for the moment it was still housed within a Victorian building; ornate red brickwork on the outside and tiles in various shades of green on the inside. A new lift had been installed, presumably replacing one of those huge black cages with slatted clanging gates, which was just as well, since Florence was in no mood to climb stairs.

She was by now bent over in discomfort and clutching her belly. Jonas helped her to the lift, her hospital bag slung over his shoulder. They went to the third floor and located Lister ward, named, as Jonas explained, after the man who had introduced carbolic acid to hospitals and thus virtually eliminated post-natal deaths due to puerperal fever. Unsurprisingly, Florence wasn't listening.

At the nurses' station an imposing West Indian staff nurse greeted them.

"I think I'm in labour," Florence told her. "I'm Mrs McManus.

"Oh yes, we've been expecting you" replied the nurse. "Come along with me and I'll show you to your bed."

She strode off down the corridor with Florence and Jonas close behind. They entered a four-bedded room and the staff nurse indicated that Florence was to have one of the beds by the window. "Here we are dearie, this is your bed. Now you just put this gown on and I'll come back and examine you."

Florence looked sheepishly at Jonas, feeling desperately nervous now things were underway and she had been absorbed into the hospital system. Jonas pulled round the bed screens and helped her to undress and get into the gown. She then went off to locate the bathroom, while he tidied away her street clothes. The other beds in the room were empty and there was just a gentle hum of air conditioning.

He peered out of the window. It was just starting to get dark, but he could make out the buildings of the adjacent London Road campus of Reading University, a much larger university than his own.

Suddenly the silence was shattered by a loud and prolonged yell of pain from somewhere on the floor below, and Jonas began to perspire. The serious business of childbirth was happening somewhere not too far away.

Florence appeared at the door of the room, clutching her washbag. "Did you hear that?" she asked nervously and reached out to take his hand, squeezing it tightly. "I don't want to do this. I'm frightened, Jonas."

So was Jonas, but he knew he had to be brave for her sake. "It'll be OK, I'll be with you all the way" he said, hugging her tightly.

"I think I might sit on the bed and wait for the midwife" she replied. "The pains have stopped for the moment, I hope I haven't put a stop to everything."

Just then the staff nurse returned with an instrument tray and began putting on a pair of latex gloves. "Right let's see how far you are along, you lie down on the bed and we'll get these curtains around for a bit of privacy."

She carried out an internal examination, then listened to the baby's heart using her foetal stethoscope. "You're two fingers dilated, so we'll just have to wait a while for baby to make a bid for freedom" she said, laughing at her own joke. "Baby seems to be full of fight, so it shouldn't be long. Just press the bedside call button if you need help." With that she opened the curtains to Jonas. "Now, you just keep on rubbing her back and taking her mind off the pain," she told him, and bustled out of the room.

And that was what Jonas did for the next three hours. The contractions became more frequent and the pain got worse, with Florence beginning to swear under her breath and squeezing his hand ever more tightly. He felt somewhat useless, since the back rubbing didn't seem to help much and there was only so much he could do to offer reassurance and encouragement. He was also beginning to feel really hungry.

They had left in such a hurry that he hadn't thought to make a sandwich or a drink.

The staff nurse returned and decided Florence was only making slow progress. "Three fingers now, so some progress, but I think it'll be a while yet so I'll give you some pethidine for the pain" she said. She administered the pethidine, then left them again.

Soon Florence was asleep and snoring gently. Jonas listened to the gentle sound for an hour, then decided to risk a short absence and went off in search of a drinks machine. He eventually found both drinks and snacks dispensers in the basement, and clutching a cup of coffee and a bag of crisps he returned to the ward, feeling guilty that he had left Florence alone, even though she was asleep.

However, in his absence things had moved on. Florence had awoken to terrible pain. She was also lying in a puddle, having wet herself, and now she wanted to pass a gigantic poo. Clutching for the call bell, she screamed for assistance. "I need a bedpan NOW please! Can somebody come?"

Through blurred vision and a befuddled mind she was suddenly aware that she was being manhandled into a wheelchair and pushed at some speed out of the room and down the corridor into a room that looked like a miniature operating theatre, with a central flat table and overhead bright lights. In an instant she was on the table, knees up, legs apart and pushing like mad. She now realised at last that it wasn't a giant poo she was about to deliver but a baby.

Jonas meanwhile had returned to the room to find that

Florence had disappeared. He immediately realised what had happened and sought the staff nurse at the main desk.

"I think my wife must have gone to the labour room," he blurted out. "Can I go and join her?"

"Yes, but be quick, she looked as if she was in a hurry. You should find her in room 304."

Jonas needed no further encouragement and dashed off. Within a few seconds he was at the door of room 304, where he could hear Florence shouting "Why don't they tell you it's going to hurt like hell! Arghh!"

Jonas burst into the room to see a midwife bent between Florence's knees. "One more heave Florence, the head's out, just got to get these shoulders through." And with what seemed like the roar of a wild beast, Florence pushed their new baby into the world.

"Grrrrrr - bloody fucking hell, grrrrrr! Oh I'm so sorry. Grrrrr!"

Jonas watched as a bloody vernix-covered shape slithered into the midwife's hands. "You've got a beautiful baby girl Florence" she said, holding the baby for Florence and Jonas to see. Florence immediately burst into tears and Jonas followed suit. Their baby daughter looked gorgeous, despite the blood and vernix.

"Oh look Florence, she's smiling- she's going to be a rascal like her mother" said Jonas. He gave Florence a big hug while the midwife took the baby away to clean and weigh her.

"Well done, was it too awful?"

Florence wept uncontrollably. "Yes it was, but I'm so

happy and she's so gorgeous."

The midwife brought the baby back, wrapped now in a pink hospital blanket. "Do you have a name for her?" she enquired as she handed the bundle over to Florence.

"I think we agreed on Cordelia," Florence told her. Jonas nodded.

"Right, why don't you see if Cordelia will take the breast"

Florence fumbled with the opening of her gown and held Cordelia to her left breast, and in a flash the little mouth was rooting and then sucking at her nipple.

"She won't get any milk for a start, but it's important that she gets the colostrum that you will produce. Just let her suck at both breasts for as long as she likes. I'll come back and bring you a bowl so you can have a wash."

She left Florence and Jonas to enjoy baby Cordelia. Their tears had dried and they were both overwhelmed with feelings of joy and happiness and a sense of wonderment over the new life they had created.

CHAPTER FIVE

SLEEPLESS NIGHTS AND FULL-ON DAYS

Jonas was running along a seemingly endless corridor towards a patch of light at its end. He was aware of a piercing crying sound which he couldn't place. It seemed inhuman, like a small animal in pain. Suddenly it was right beside him, and he felt an elbow nudging him. He turned to see who was doing the nudging and woke to see Florence with Cordelia on her left breast.

"Come on Mr Sleepy, you're on duty once she's had both sides, so you might as well go and make us a cup of tea" she said. Jonas pulled himself upright in the bed and rubbed the sleep out of his eyes. He felt very groggy, for this was the second rude awakening of the night.

"Haven't you told her I have to go to work in the morning?"

"Yes, and she said academics don't do real work, and especially in your case. You just go to work to play with your oversized chemistry set."

Jonas grunted and heaved himself out of bed. "Well, someone's been feeding her lies. She'll understand when her daddy is a famous chemist."

"That'll be the day. Now off you go, I need to keep up my fluid intake."

Jonas went downstairs and made the tea and a couple of slices of toast. It was 4 am, not a good time to be woken, because the chances were you would not get back to sleep. By the time he returned with the tray, Cordelia was asleep on Florence's right breast. They left her there while they had their tea and toast.

"Breast milk: free of charge and comes in cute little packages," he observed. "Though in your case, not so small."

"Well keep your hands off them, they belong to Cordelia now."

"She gets all the fun."

Florence handed their daughter over as soon as he had finished his tea. "OK, she's all yours, don't forget to wind her after you've changed her."

"Yes boss," he grunted and carried Cordelia into their second bedroom, where they had her changing mat and Moses basket. Jonas was now quite an accomplished nappy changer. The trick after a breast feed was to judge the exact moment to remove the old nappy. Sure enough, after a couple of minutes of winding, there was the unmistakeable sound of a yellow squitter being squeezed into the old nappy. He waited a further minute to make sure Cordelia had finished, then undid the tapes on the nappy to reveal the liquid, bright yellow mess. He was completely unfazed by this and quickly removed and wrapped the dirty nappy, cleaned her bottom, applied zinc and castor oil cream then wrapped her in her new nappy. The dirty one could wait for morning before disposal.

Now the serious business of winding had to commence.

Laziness in this activity inevitably led to the colic and no further sleep for anyone, so he placed Cordelia over his shoulder and rubbed her back gently until a small burp emerged. He continued rubbing for a few minutes more, then laid her gently in her basket. With any luck she would sleep until seven.

Florence was snoring gently when he got back to their bedroom, and had spread herself diagonally across the mattress. Jonas pushed her gently away from his side and climbed in beside her. She stirred and grunted: "You're cold, did she settle?"

"Yes, now move over a bit, I've barely got room for one leg, let alone two."

She snuggled up to him and began to breathe deeply almost immediately. He wriggled around until he got comfortable and soon began to drift away; but Cordelia was not going to allow him to have things that easy. First she began to snuffle and root around and then to whimper, and finally she let loose a piercing cry. Jonas and Florence both started in response.

"You obviously didn't wind her properly," Florence mumbled.

"Perhaps you didn't give her enough milk."

"No, she had 15 minutes on each side, it must be her colic. Give her a teaspoon of gripe water."

Jonas heaved himself out of bed and went to find the gripe water. After some minutes of searching he found it on the bathroom shelf in among the shampoos, Cutex nail varnish remover and next to a box of Tampax, not yet in use. Now for a spoon. He didn't want to have to plod all the way downstairs. Why hadn't they left one in the gripe water box? Cordelia was by now yelling her head off.

Desperate moments need imaginative measures. Jonas unscrewed the bottle cap and held it under the hot tap until the water ran really hot, then quickly went to the bedroom to pluck Cordelia from her basket. Somehow he managed to cradle her in one arm while pouring gripe water into the bottle cap he had balanced on the basket side. She willingly took the capful of Dinnefords and smacked her lips contentedly. The crying stopped immediately and she lay quietly in his arms as he rocked her gently.

Soon she began to breathe more deeply and her eyelids flickered as she began to dream. Jonas placed her carefully into the basket and covered her with her pink blanket. He crept back to bed, pleased with himself and pleased that they had accepted (somewhat reluctantly) the advice of Florence's mother about the use of gripe water. Their attempts to bring up a drug-free baby were already in tatters.

Cordelia slept on until around seven before she woke Florence and Jonas for her morning feed. Jonas felt a little sleep-deprived, but he had a quiet day ahead of him so was not too bothered. One lecture at eleven, then a lab class to supervise in the afternoon. He made them both some tea and toast while Florence fed Cordelia.

"Well done," Florence praised him. "Did she take the Dinnefords OK?"

"Yes, she seemed to like it."

"I meant to leave a spoon in the box, sorry to make you drag all the way downstairs."

"She took it from the bottle cap." Jonas knew he should have kept his mouth shut even as the words emerged from his lips

Florence's astonishment was matched by her obvious annoyance. "She did what? You lazy bugger!"

"Well it worked OK, that's what matters."

"And what about the germs on the bottle cap?"

"I washed it under the hot tap."

"Well, don't do it again!"

Jonas knew she was right, but he still felt unfairly admonished. He went to the bathroom and ran a bath. Not a good start to the day.

Once he was dressed, he offered to make them both some porridge, but Florence declined, so he settled for two slices of toast with peanut butter spread and another cup of tea. Florence seemed to have forgotten his transgression when he returned to the bedroom before leaving for work. She was in the middle of changing Cordelia, who had done yet another yellow squitter.

"She seems to get rid of your milk as soon as you give it to her, "Jonas observed.

"Well hopefully her little tummy has managed to extract some goodness from it on the way through. You off then?"

"Yeah, I shouldn't be late, I'll give you a ring around lunchtime." He kissed her on the cheek, but she turned to kiss him on the lips. "Sorry I was short with you, but you are a lazy sod, like all men!"

"I know, it's in our genes." He gave her a squeeze. "Love you madly, have fun with Cordelia."

"Hurry home to us."

★ ★ ★ ★ ★

Although Jonas got to the department by eight, Samantha was already in and waiting for him. "Dr McManus, I've got some bad news. Professor Courtney-Jones has rung in to say that he has been summoned to the BBC to talk about his latest results on lead and intelligence." She paused briefly to see if Jonas had anticipated what was coming next, but he was taken by surprise. "He has a nine o'clock lecture with the first years and he wants you to give it for him."

She could see that he was wondering what the hell he was going to talk about.

"I've dug out the relevant lecture notes for you, he has marked where he got to last time." She handed Jonas a large file. Jonas sighed audibly. What a huge imposition, and only an hour to think about what he had to say.

"Thanks a million, you've really made my day!"

"I knew you'd be pleased" she said, and grinned at him. "It could have been worse, Dr Lewis has picked up his eleven o'clock lecture to the second year bioscientists. At least your first year chemists will sit quietly and listen to you rather than chatter and throw things!"

"Well that's a blessing, thanks for your kind greeting, I'll remember to slip in the back way tomorrow."

"But I'll still come and find you!" She rushed off back to her office.

Jonas let himself into his office and opened up the file. Although the handwritten notes had originally been neat and well-ordered, each page was heavily annotated with phrases and whole sentences in a variety of colours. The overall appearance was certainly colourful, as if a child had gained access to the notes and had used the pages as a substitute for a colouring book. Where to start?

Jonas noted that two pages were held together with a small bulldog clip. At the foot of the first of these pages, Courtney-Jones had written 'finished here Nov 29th'. The page was covered with structures of simple acetylenes; he had obviously been talking about basic acetylene chemistry.

Jonas unclipped the pages and read on. It was all basic stuff, complete with anecdotes about early investigators and industrial uses. Jonas heaved a sigh of relief. The task was not going to be as onerous as he had feared.

In the event, the lecture went well, though he was initially taken aback when he walked into the ground floor lecture theatre to discover more than two hundred first year students staring down at him from a dozen or so rows of seats in the steeply-raked theatre. Several more arrived during the first ten minutes, and there was much breakfast-eating during his lecture, but all dutifully took at least some notes as he tried to be animated by Courtney-Jones' material. One student did pluck up courage and ask a question about his use of the term 'alkynes', as Courtney-Jones had always talked about acetylenes. Jonas realised that he should have used the older word, since Courtney-Jones was an old-school chemist, and he explained that the two terminologies could be used interchangeably. But overall, it went satisfactorily, and he escaped back to his office at 9.50 feeling well pleased with his 'baptism by fire'.

Rob Lewis knocked on his door ten minutes later. "Hear you picked up one of our leader's lectures at nine," he said, grinning broadly.

"Yep, and you've got the one at eleven."

"Oh that's easy, the biochemists don't usually turn up, and if they do they just sit and doodle for fifty minutes. It doesn't really matter what you tell them."

"Do these lecture swaps happen very often?"

Rob Lewis smiled. "More and more frequently. He's becoming quite a telly personality now that the media sense that he's onto something with this lead and intelligence business. The oil companies are hopping made."

"Yes he is rather undermining their cheap and nasty way of perking up their petrol."

"Anyway, see you later. We're sharing the first year lab class this afternoon."

After he had left, Jonas started to look at his notes for the eleven o'clock lecture. He had worked on them over the weekend and was pretty clear about what he was going to say. This was a second year class of chemists and he was going to talk to them about natural products chemistry, his own favourite subject, so he was actually looking forward to the lecture. The actor in him relished the thought of standing in front of an audience and reading his lines with a theatrical flourish.

The reality was somewhat disappointing, since his audience only numbered around a dozen; it had been a very poor year for admissions. His theatrical skills were not needed and he barely had to raise his voice in the tiny lecture theatre. The students were initially very attentive, since he represented something new and potentially interesting, but they soon settled into their usual mode of yawning, coughing and paper shuffling.

A couple of the boys and one of the girls did seem genuinely interested in what he was talking about, and at the end the girl stayed behind to talk to him. She had long black hair and huge brown gazelle eyes, and a figure that was accentuated by her mini skirt and tight ribbed top. Jonas could not help being flattered that she had stayed behind.

"You said morphine probably protects the opium poppy from being eaten, but if it is poisonous, why doesn't it harm the plant?" she enquired.

"Good question, and the answer is that it is mainly stored in little sacs or vesicles that only release the morphine when an insect or herbivore bites into the plant."

"Oh, I see. And how did humans discover the 'druggy' effects of morphine?"

"No one knows, but I guess by a process of trial and error."

"By eating the plant?"

Jonas spent a few minutes explaining that most of the morphine was contained in the unripe seed capsules and would have had to be collected and processed before consumption. She seemed interested, though perhaps he had overdone his explanations, because she suddenly stifled a yawn. "Oh, I'm sorry, that was very rude of me. I had a late night." Jonas felt just the merest *soupçon* of desire and found himself wishing he had been part of her late night before crushing this lascivious thought.

"Well, if you have any more questions, feel free to come along to my office for a chat." He suggested.

"Thank you, very interesting lecture."

You only needed one bright and beautiful student to make it all worthwhile.

It was by now 12.15 and he decided to try the Senior Common Room for lunch. This Victorian house was just across the lawn from the Chemistry Department and was one of the few original buildings still left on the campus. Most of the front part was taken up with a large lounge complete with bar, and he immediately spotted Rob Lewis leaning against the bar with a pint in his hand.

"You survived the ordeal then," Rob asked. "My lot were mostly still asleep at eleven and several actually left before the end. The bioscientists can't see the point of chemistry. Can't say I blame them, who needs it if you're into farm animals or marine worms?"

"My first years were very docile, why are there so many of them?" asked Jonas.

"Oh the university makes all students in the Faculties of Science and Agriculture take chemistry in their first year. Load of nonsense and the students hate it, but it helps our numbers. We couldn't justify our existence without them."

Jonas reached into his pocket for some money, but Rob, observing this move, offered to buy him a drink.

"What d'you fancy? The Brakespeare bitter is very good, little local brewery."

"I'd better just have a half, don't want to be caught drunk in charge of a lab this afternoon."

Rob laughed out loud. "Nonsense, it's only bearable if you're slightly pissed. Let me have another pint please Bernard."

Jonas hadn't really noticed the barman until that moment. He had the appearance of an ex-RAF type with his handlebar moustache and slightly aloof military bearing.

"Haven't seen you in here before, are you a new member of staff?" he asked, offering his hand for Jonas to shake.

"Yes, just started today in Chemistry."

"Not many of your lot ever come across to the SCR, all a bit too serious for my liking, apart from Dr Lewis here, and he's a regular" he smirked.. Jonas took the newly-drawn pint and raised it to his lips. "Cheers Rob, here's to a nice quiet lab class."

"Oh, you don't want that! Far too boring. A few fires, the odd bit of broken glass tubing rammed into the hand, a girl fainting from the fumes. That's what you need to pass the time. You'll see. The first year lab class is always the best because they're all so inept!"

Before Jonas could think up a response, they were joined

by a tall, well-built man in his early forties who seemed to ooze self-confidence.

"Hello Rob, going to buy me a drink?"

"No, you owe me one, and any way you're a Senior Lecturer so you can easily afford to buy me one." Then as an aside: "By the way, this is Jonas McManus, our new young whizzkid. Jonas, this is John Brewer, but we all call him Basher. He's from Social Sciences."

"So whatyer doing at this godawful place if you're such a whizzo?" he asked with a guffaw. "Sorry, only joking."

"Well firstly I'm no whiz, and secondly it was the only job going. What's your speciality?"

Rob didn't give him chance to respond. "He's ex-police and teaches about criminality. He knows all of the local low-life and joins in all their fights just for the fun of it, hence his nickname."

Brewer punched Rob on the shoulder, obviously with some force, because Rob winced. "Don't believe a word that this dipso Scot tells you, he's full of bullshit" he said

"But do you teach Criminality?" asked Jonas.

"Yes I do, but I escape from this dump as often as I can, research trips whenever I can get the money." He ordered his drink, took a large draught, then continued: "Just back from Colombia in fact."

Jonas expressed genuine surprise and interest: "Wow, that must have been amazing, how did you swing that one?"

"I persuaded the Met to send me on a fact-finding mission about the cocaine trade." Brewer was obviously very pleased with himself. "Boy it's a mess out there, like the Wild West with hit-men from the various drugs cartels bumping off politicians and cops whenever the mood takes them."

"Weren't you worried?" Jonas asked him.

"Yep, in the end I asked one question too many and had to be escorted to the airport for a flight home. The cops said I'd be dead in 24 hours if I didn't leave."

"Makes the afternoon practical class we're about to look after seem like a vicar's tea party," laughed Rob.

"And it also makes our local criminals seem very tame," Brewer observed.

"Do you know many of them?" Jonas enquired.

Again Brewer seemed particularly full of himself. "Just a few. Well a chap needs to get his drugs from somewhere!" He laughed heartily, slapping Rob on the shoulder again. "You should give up the booze Rob and become a druggie, much better for your old liver."

"No thanks, I don't fancy a spell in Wormwood Scrubs."

Brewer drained his glass and gathered up the pile of papers he had deposited on the bar.

"Nice to meet you Jonas, got to give these essays back to my third year students. Read them on the plane home from Colombia, mostly a pile of poo. See you Rob, think about my advice."

There was a moment's silence after he left, then Rob delivered his character assassination.

"He's the biggest bullshitter in the university. Does bugger all in Social Sciences but manages to get piles of money for his trips. And he does seem to be in with the local criminal fraternity, says he needs to bring his first hand experience to bear on his teaching. Not that he seems to do much of that. He's your typical lazy academic!"

Rob also drained his glass and rose from his bar stool.

"Time to join the fray laddie, first year practical awaits."

At two o'clock Jonas donned his new white lab coat and joined Rob Lewis in the large sixty-person laboratory which occupied the entire 'stick' of their T-shaped building. Students of all shapes and sizes and colours were entering from the opposite end, where the spiral staircase deposited them.

"Find your bench from the list on the wall," Rob shouted down the lab. "You should already have received a copy of the lab manual and you should have read the entries on safety and experiment one, benzoylation of a phenol."

During the next five minutes there was much milling around, opening of bench drawers, idle chatter and most disconcerting of all, puzzled looks as the students read about the experiment for the first time.

"None of them will have read up on their first experiment, so we can expect some fun and games" Rob informed Jonas with a wry grin. "The boys will be sloppy and the girls will be nervous, they'll need a helping hand." He winked at Jonas.

And so it turned out. Each student had been assigned a phenol of unknown structure and had to mix it with sodium hydroxide solution and benzoyl chloride in a test tube to make a crystalline derivative whose melting point would indicate the identity of the phenol. All very straightforward, but this apparent simplicity obscured two problems for the uninitiated. Benzoyl chloride is a lachrymatory liquid and the thick-walled test tube in the kit of glassware possessed a ground glass stopper that was easily confused with a tubular adaptor with a ground glass joint at each end. About ten per cent of the students used the tubular adaptor instead of the stopper when shaking their mixture, with the result that the contents of the test tube erupted out of the tube and were deposited on them or their neighbour. One particularly aggressive shaker managed to send his mixture two whole rows away. While only a small number of students spilt their mixtures, the lachrymatory properties of the benzoyl chloride soon had everyone in tears.

"Why don't you tell them to carry out the reactions in the fume cupboards?" Jonas asked Rob after his umpteenth mission of mercy with lachrymose and disconcerted students.

"Have you seen our fume cupboards?" replied Lewis. "There's not enough to go round, and there's no suck on them any way."

Jonas was kept busy helping students to carry out the experiment properly, never sure whether the student tears were chemically induced or due to frustration. In the end most of the students obtained a crystalline benzoate, which they then had to purify by recrystallization from methylated spirits. This involved dissolving the crude benzoate in hot meths, then allowing the solution to cool, thus inducing crystallisation. The lab manual clearly indicated the use of a steambath as the source of heat, but students don't read lab manuals and a number used a Bunsen burner, tripod and gauze to heat the solution. Mostly they were lucky, but two girls managed to knock over their solutions, then announced the resultant fires with their screams. Jonas extinguished one of the fires and Rob dealt with the other, giving the girl he had saved a big hug to calm her down.

"I told you this class was fun," Rob reminded him once the dramas were over. "You get to squeeze prime young flesh!"

At the end of three hours, Jonas was exhausted. He was only too glad to escape along with the students out into the fresh air and away from the department, but he knew he stank of chemicals. Florence met him at the front door, Cordelia asleep in her arms.

"God, you stink! Go straight upstairs and have a bath, you're not getting near me or Cordelia till you've washed the stink of that department off you!" Jonas did as he was told.

Later over dinner, salmon bake and broccoli, he asked her about her day. "We explored the lower half of the Wokingham Road, the shops and the primary school" said Florence, rocking Cordelia, who was half asleep on her lap and just beginning to whimper, since it was almost time for her early evening feed. "There's a load of interesting shops. An old-fashioned greengrocer with fruit and vegetables in boxes and two bakeries. One's run by a lovely old West Indian man called Hot John. I found two Asian supermarkets, and there are three newsagents, would you believe."

"Did you get anything?"

"Only a jam doughnut from Hot John because I was peckish, but guess what, I did an awful thing."

"Sang a calypso with Hot John?"

"No, don't be stupid! I left Cordelia outside Hot John's in her pram and started to walk back up the hill without her!"

"How on earth could you have done that?"

"Just a moment's forgetfulness, not being used to being out with a baby in a pram. But it did give me a fright and I went into a cold sweat. I'd only gone a hundred yards before I remembered, and when I got back to her Hot John was peering into the pram and cooing at her. I felt so stupid."

Jonas reached over and took her hand. "No harm done. I bet you don't do it again."

"No, it was really scary. Perhaps my post-natal hormones have made me forgetful."

Jonas had finished his dinner, so Florence passed Cordelia across the table to him.

"I'll just finish my dinner and then feed her" she said. "What about your day?"

Jonas started to rock the now whimpering Cordelia. "Oh fine, but pretty full-on. I arrived to find that Courtney-Jones had buggered off for the day, so I had to give his lecture for him. Then the lab class this afternoon was full of novice students who didn't know how to do anything and spilled lots of lachrymatory chemicals. Made an awful stink."

"What did you do for lunch?"

"Oh I had a pint with Rob Lewis, the slightly alcoholic Scot I told you about, and I met this cocky bloke from Social Sciences who's an expert on the local criminals and the Colombian drug trade. Interesting but a bit full of himself."

Florence relieved him of Cordelia and began to breastfeed her.

"Your colleagues do seem to be an odd lot, still, you're a bit of a geek so it must be an academic thing."

"That's a bit unfair, just because you switch off if I start to talk chemistry doesn't make me a geek. But I agree that they are a strange crowd. Courtney-Jones has got such a bee in his bonnet about lead in petrol, he's making himself very unpopular with the oil companies."

"Well I think he's doing a great job, I don't want Cordelia breathing in nasty lead fumes." She handed her over to Jonas. "Now you give her a good winding and I'll make us a cup of tea."

Jonas began to rub and pat Cordelia's tiny back, waiting for the inevitable explosion of liquid poo that always followed the first half of her feed. He was not disappointed. She obliged just as Florence came back to the table with two mugs of tea.

"She's just done her early evening squitter," Jonas informed her. "Shall I go and change her?"

"No have your tea, she'll probably do some more any way."

Jonas carried on with the winding. Florence put his mug down on the table, then gave him a peck on the cheek. "I'm sorry I've been out of action, I'm still a bit sore down below" she said.

"That's OK, I do understand, it can't have been easy squeezing out this little bundle."

"I don't want you getting moody on me because you can't have it."

"What, me? Besides I've got all these gorgeous girl students fighting over me."

She punched him on the arm. "In your dreams! Now give that baby to me and I'll clear up this poo."

CHAPTER SIX

THE DANGERS OF CHEMISTRY

Their social life had been non-existent since Cordelia arrived, until Noel Grimwold invited them for lunch. He lived with his wife and daughter in a converted pub in the village of Oaktrees Common, a few miles from Reading. Although Jonas had received good directions, they made several wrong turns while negotiating the extremely narrow lanes and had to reverse for several hundred yards when suddenly confronted by a tractor whose ruddy-faced driver was not going to give way. But eventually they found the house with its picket fence and small front garden, full of Spring flowers.

Jonas banged on the door knocker while Florence was getting Cordelia out of the car. The door swung open almost at once and Noel appeared, his thick shock of grey hair apparently uncombed and an overlarge butcher's apron wrapped around his small frame.

"Hey, you've caught me on the hop, Brigitte isn't back yet from her friend's birthday bash. She promised she'd be back after breakfast to help with the lunch."

Florence appeared at Jonas' side, Cordelia asleep in her carry cot.

"Oh I hope we haven't come too early," Jonas began, handing Noel the bottle of red wine they had brought, "but you did say 12.30."

"No, no not at all, I've got everything under control. She'll be here soon. Come in and meet Claudette." At that moment a pretty six or seven-year-old (Jonas guessed) with a mass of dark brown curls came bounding up to the door. "Daddy are these your friends from work?"

"Yes love, this is Jonas and Florence and their new baby Cordelia. Come on in and I'll get some drinks."

They stepped into a large room which had presumably been the public bar of the pub, and the original dark stained wooden bar faced them on the far side of the room. Behind the bar the shelves which would have held glasses and bottles now bore a vast collection of jugs and countless other bits of pottery, including what looked like a Clarice Cliffe crocus coffee set.

"Come through the bar and you can watch me while I cook our lunch, if you don't mind."

"No not all, is there anything I can do?" asked Florence, handing the carrycot to Jonas.

"No thanks, I think I've got everything under control, it's only a casserole and everything's in the pot ready to go in the oven. Let me get you a glass of something."

They entered a large kitchen and Noel went to the fridge. "I've got white wine or homebrew, and of course a good Côtes du Rhone, that's where Brigitte hails from."

"I'd like a small glass of white wine," asked Florence.

"And I'd like a glass of Côtes du Rhone," said Jonas. "Can I put Cordelia somewhere quiet until she wakes for her feed?"

"Of course. Claudette, why don't you take Jonas to the spare bedroom?"

Jonas followed Claudette up a narrow staircase to a smallish bedroom and put the carrycot carefully onto the bed. The upstairs was considerably smaller than the downstairs, which suggested that this had been a country pub rather than an inn.

"Do you want to see my room?" Claudette asked him. "It's really pretty."

"Yes, that would be great." She led him down a narrow corridor to a slightly larger bedroom which, like the other one, had a low ceiling and walls that had a slight curve and were very irregular. The room was totally pink and seemed to be full of dolls of all sizes and colours.

"Wow, you've got a great collection of dolls," observed Jonas. Do you have a favourite one?"

"This is Marianne, she's French and my mummy got her for me." Claudette handed him a large doll with an attractive smile and long blonde hair. The doll was exquisitely dressed in a pink frock with many pleats and bows and fine lacy underwear to complement her dress.

"She's very pretty, your mummy chose very well" he said.

"She has her own bed and I don't allow her to come in my bed because Mummy says we shouldn't get her into bad habits," Claudette informed him earnestly. Jonas had exhausted his small talk on the subject of dolls and was keen to rejoin Florence. "I'm sure that's very sensible" he said. "Now shall we go down and see if your dad needs any help?"

They rejoined Florence and Noel in the kitchen, and Jonas noticed that Florence was somewhat squeezed into a corner with Noel almost touching her. She turned and raised her eyebrows as soon as they made eye contact, and Noel moved away towards the large oven.

"Must get this casserole cooking" he said. He reached for a heavy red Le Creuset casserole and depressed the oven door handle with his knee. "Could you open the door for me Florence, please?"

Florence pulled open the door so Noel could insert the casserole on the highest shelf. "Now I wonder where that wife of mine has got to, she's so forgetful" he muttered. "Let's go and sit in the conservatory and have our drinks."

He led the way through to a large conservatory attached to the back wall of the bar. Through the windows they could see the small cottage garden displaying a profusion of multi-coloured Spring flowers.

"Someone likes gardening," Florence observed.

"Oh it's mainly me, I'm afraid," Noel said. "Brigitte is always far too busy attending folk groups or acting as a special constable at weekends."

"What!" exclaimed Jonas, "A special constable, why on earth does she do that?"

"I think she likes the uniform and the incredulous looks she gets from drunks when she talks to them with a French accent."

As if on cue, they heard the front door open and someone called out: "Noel, Claudette, I am 'ome, 'ave you meesed me?"

Noel raised his bushy eyebrows. "We're in the conservatory,

darling" he called. A smallish woman with huge hair and a highly patterned peasant skirt and white blouse appeared at the entrance to the conservatory. Claudette rushed over to her.

"Mummy, mummy, Daddy's friends have come to see us!"

"Oh 'ow nice, we 'ave guests, I must go and change."

"Don't you dare!" Noel warned her. "I told you Florence and Jonas were coming, and you were supposed to be here to help me with the lunch."

"I'm so sorry *cherie*, I'll go and prepare something at once." Again Noel looked despairingly at his wife. "It's all in hand. I've made a *coq au vin* and it's in the oven. Now get yourself a glass of wine and come and sit down."

"Oh that's so nice, friends for lunch and notheeng to do."

There was definitely something of the mad Frenchwoman about her, Jonas mused. She had that twinkle in her eye and air of abstraction that he associated with someone who was living on a slightly different level from everyone else. She returned with a glass of white wine and sat next to Jonas on the two-seater sofa, immediately putting her hand on his knee.

"Now tell me who are theez lovely people?"

"Let me remind you," Noel told her with an air of exasperation, "this is Jonas, our new lecturer, and his lovely wife Florence, who is a nurse, and their new baby girl is asleep upstairs."

Brigitte squeezed Jonas' knee. "Oh you are so clevair, just like Noel, to make a baby girl. I so love baby girls. And what eez she named?"

"Cordelia," Florence informed her.

"Oh so nice, one of the characters in that famous book *Pride of Prepuce.*" Noel snorted with laughter and Jonas smirked, but Florence set her straight.

"*King Lear* actually, by William Shakespeare."

"Oh yes, I'm so ignorant of your literature."

Then she turned to Noel. "I had such a good time with Babette *cherie*, we shopped in the Kings Road, how do you say, we shopped till we were dropped, and on the way back to 'er 'ouse on the tube these two lovely young men tried to seduce us. They wanted to take us to a club and they both had their arms round us until Babette told them I was in the police and they just left. It was such fun!"

"Like I've always said, you're not safe to be let out on the streets" Noel scolded her. He left to check on his lunch preparations.

"Tell us about your job as a special constable," Jonas suggested.

"Oh eets notheeng, mostly picking up girls who have fallen over after too much drink, and breaking up the boys who are fighting, I only work on Friday evenings, eet's so much more fun."

"It sounds dangerous to me," observed Florence. "Aren't you worried about getting hurt?" Noel came back into the conservatory. "She always goes around with this really huge full-time policeman called Ted, so there's little chance of that. And like I said, the drunks and brawlers are always so surprised to hear a foreign voice they soon start to behave."

They were all suddenly aware of a baby's cry from upstairs.

"I'll get her," said Florence and she went off to collect Cordelia with Claudette in close pursuit. Brigitte held up her glass for a refill as Noel poured more wine into Jonas' glass.

"Oh I forgot to tell you," Brigitte began. "Last Friday we saw that funny man you call Smasher or something."

"You mean John Brewer, Basher, from Sociology."

"Yes him, they came to dinner once, his wife wears white socks and big sandals. A very funny woman."

"I met him at lunch the other day," recalled Jonas. "He claimed he knew all the local drug dealers."

Brigitte nodded. "He was talking to a couple of 'ard men that Ted said were real druggies. I said hello just so he'd know I 'ad seen him, but he didn't seem to recognise me."

"He's a funny bloke," observed Noel. "He came to see me the other day to ask if I could make him some speed, you know methedrine. I told him I valued my job too much to start making hard drugs. Borrowing helium cylinders is one thing, but at least it's not illegal. He's a dangerous bloke."

Florence reappeared, carrying Cordelia. "OK if I sit and feed her? She'd done a poo and that woke her up but I think she's hungry too."

"Of course, it's so lovely to see them feed, I so enjoyed feeding Claudette," observed Brigitte.

Florence opened her blouse and very discreetly lowered her bra and placed Cordelia on her breast. Claudette came over and got very close so that she could see what was happening.

"Oh Mummy, she really likes it."

"Of course she does *cherie*, you used to love it too."

Noel and Brigitte both got up and left the conservatory. "I'll just set the table," said Brigitte. "Noel can finish getting his dinner ready."

Claudette stroked Cordelia's cheek. "Does it tickle when she sucks your boobie?" she asked Florence.

Florence laughed. "Well it tickles a bit and sometimes she gives me a bit of a nip with her gums. But mostly it's just a lovely warm feeling as she takes the milk."

"My friend Tanya, her Mum says that feeding babies makes you get small boobies, so she didn't feed Tanya. But I think that's sad. I'm glad I had booby."

"I think you're so right," Florence told her. "Who wants big boobies anyway?" She looked across at Jonas.

"Don't look at me, I like them any way they come."

Further discussion of the merits of boob size and breast feeding was interrupted by the return of Brigitte, who asked them to come through to the dining room for lunch. A mid-size refectory table had been covered with a large, elaborately-cut lace tablecloth, probably French, Florence guessed, and set with large basic cutlery, again very French. They took their places after Florence had handed Cordelia to Jonas for winding, and he sat for the moment in an armchair to one side of the table. Noel appeared at the door with his casserole, which he set down in the centre of the table.

"I'm afraid it's got a bit overcooked, but I think it will taste OK" he said. He proceeded to serve the rather dark mixture onto the five plates placed between the five sets of cutlery. It was rather hard to distinguish between the brown chicken pieces and the onions and tomatoes, but the aroma of the sauce was very good.

"Help yourselves to potatoes and carrots" Noel invited them as he sat down. "I've opened the nice bottle of cabernet sauvignon that you brought, but there's plenty of white wine too."

Jonas joined the others at the table, with Cordelia lying lengthwise across his lap. They all served themselves with vegetables, accepted more wine and began to eat.

"Hey, this is really good" said Jonas. Despite the slightly burnt taste of the sauce, the *coq au vin* was indeed surprisingly good. Jonas ate with relish and since he was very hungry, filled his mouth too full. He knew Florence would make some comment later.

"Yes, very good *cherie*" said Brigitte. They ate in silence for a while, then Noel asked Jonas for his first impressions of Courtney-Jones.

"I haven't seen that much of him, he's always rushing from place to place" said Jonas.

"His wife is the same," Brigitte interposed. "She rushes round the village like a, 'ow do you say, cat out of 'ell."

"Bat out of hell," Noel corrected her. "She does seem to organise a lot of charity tea parties and jumble sales."

"He's obviously very intense about this lead in petrol business," observed Jonas.

Cordelia then began to whimper, so Florence left the table to give her the other side, and Claudette followed her into the next room to observe some more breast feeding.

"He's really upsetting the oil companies" Jonas went on.

"Every time he goes on TV he gets a flurry of abusive mail from the oil industry. Some politicians have begun to grumble that he is disturbing the economy with his, they claim, unsubstantiated claims."

"Perhaps they will 'ave him killed!" Brigitte speculated.

"Maybe that's the way you behave in France," Noel told her, "but not in Britain."

"God, I hope not," said Jonas. "I'd probably have to give all his lectures."

"You've been unlucky there" said Noel. "He doesn't ask me because he knows I don't use his lecture notes and teach the students all kinds of more relevant stuff."

"'E doesn't ask you because 'e doesn't like you since you stole the gas cylinder!" Having given her opinion, Brigitte rose from the table and went to the kitchen, returning minutes later with a large tart.

"You see *cherie*, I did remember people were coming. I made a *tarte au citron*."

"So you did," agreed Noel. He turned to Jonas. "You're in for a treat, her tarts are really superb."

And so it was. Some hours later, after coffee and further chat, Jonas and Florence decided they should go. "Must get Cordelia home for her bath and bed," Florence said. "Thank you very much for the super lunch, and all of your help with the nappy changing Claudette."

"You must come again when it is a bit warmer," said Noel. "Then we can sit out in the garden for our lunch."

"It's your turn to come to us next time" said Jonas, gathering up Cordelia in her carrycot. Noel and Brigitte gave them both warm embraces and several kisses on the cheeks as they got into their car, and Jonas then tried to retrace the route they had taken to get to Oaktrees Common. In the event he took a wrong turning and ended up in the next village of Rushmore End. He was just passing the church when a red Citroen 2CV shot out of a side road, right up on its suspension on one side and heading straight towards them. Jonas quickly veered up onto the pavement and the 2CV roared past them heading out of the village. Jonas only caught a glimpse of the driver but the intensely focused stare was unmistakeable; it was Courtney-Jones.

* * * * *

Jonas next saw the red 2CV first thing the next morning. He had just arrived at the Chemistry Department when Courtney-Jones tore into the car park, the car once again up on its suspension almost at an angle of 60 degrees as he took the left-hand bend and skidded into his designated parking place. Jonas quickly slipped into the student entrance by the spiral staircase as Courtney-Jones rushed up the steps to the main entrance, his briefcase swinging wildly. The omens were not good: it looked like another busy day at the TV studios with his lectures farmed out to whichever poor souls were around to deliver them.

Jonas climbed the spiral staircase and hid in one of the instrument rooms, hoping to avoid discovery. But Samantha had tracked him down within ten minutes.

"It's no good trying to hide, Dr McManus, I know all the

little bolt holes" she said. Jonas tried not to look too guilty. "As you have obviously guessed, Professor Courtney-Jones wants you. All of your colleagues have commitments this morning, or so they claim, but you have a free morning. At least you did have. I'm so sorry."

She led the way back to Courtney-Jones' office and ushered Jonas into the inner office. Courtney-Jones was wearing one of his wildest expressions, his eyes bulging below his bushy eyebrows.

"Oh Jonas, sorry to have to do this to you, but I've got this really important meeting at the House of Commons, a cross-party meeting where I hope to convince MPs of the importance of my findings about lead and intelligence." Jonas nodded. "Can you give my eleven o'clock lecture? Shouldn't be too difficult, it's on ketones and aldehydes, plenty of room for anecdotes and fun examples."

There was no time for a reply, because the phone rang. Courtney-Jones lifted the receiver. "Yes Samantha. Really! Well put him through." He covered the mouthpiece with his hand and said to Jonas: "Thames Valley Police, won't be a tick."

The caller spoke for several minutes before Courtney-Jones responded. "Well I can understand your concern, but I can assure you that none of my colleagues would participate in such a venture" he said. "I will, however, make enquiries and let you know if I discover anything. Good-bye, Chief Inspector." He put down the phone and turned to Jonas. "Absolutely absurd. He says they have information from one of their informants that someone in this department is making amphetamines, methedrine in particular. Though he did admit that the man concerned was a minor drug dealer and known to be a bit unreliable."

Jonas tried to look as nonchalant as possible. "You're right, it is absurd, you'd have to be an idiot to get involved in something like that."

"Quite so, but keep your eyes open. I hope none of the technicians is trying to supplement his meagre salary." He began rifling through the papers in his briefcase. It was clear that their meeting was at an end and that it was assumed that Jonas had agreed to give the eleven o'clock lecture.

"Has Samantha got your lecture notes?" Jonas asked.

"Oh yes, and thank you once again."

Jonas collected the notes and went straight to see Noel Grimwold. "Thanks again for the nice lunch yesterday" he said.

"Not at all, it was great seeing you all. Brigitte and Claudette were very taken with your baby daughter."

"I've just seen Courtney-Jones and he's had a call from the police. Some criminal has informed them that someone in Chemistry is making methedrine."

Noel looked genuinely shocked. "I bet it's that idiot Brewer from Sociology bragging to his druggy mates in the pub. Silly sod, he'll get us all into trouble. Just as well I told him I wasn't interested."

"I told Courtney-Jones that none of us would be so stupid as to get involved."

"Quite so, but thanks for the warning anyway."

Later, after giving Courtney-Jones' lecture, Jonas went to

see his other colleagues to let them know about the call from the police. Albert Greenough was only slightly interested, and dismissed the rumours of a department drug maker as nonsense. But when he entered Rob Lewis' office, he found him in earnest conversation with John Brewer, the alleged 'middleman' in the supposed drugs operation.

"Thought you'd like to know that the local police believe that someone in the department is making methedrine," Jonas told them. He couldn't help adding mischievously, "I don't suppose you know anything about it?" He was amused to note that they both suddenly turned quite pale, and he assumed that any involvement they might have had would cease immediately, but he was wrong.

★ ★ ★ ★ ★

Florence took Cordelia for a walk in her buggy, primarily to visit Giuseppe's delicatessen for some Parma ham and fresh Parmesan cheese. Giuseppe and his wife were serving in the shop.

"Buon giorno signora!" was the cheery greeting from Giuseppe, while his wife immediately swooped on Cordelia.

"Che bella!" she exclaimed.. She was of similar girth to her husband and, if anything, had an even more cheery and rubicund expression. Florence asked for the ham and cheese.

"We 'ave some superba pasta fresca," Giuseppe informed her, "perfetto for ravioli or cannelloni."

"OK, I'll have some of that too," Florence agreed. In the

background Radio 2 was playing quietly. She assumed it was the Jimmy Young show as it was after eleven, and sure enough as the record ended she heard the familiar voice cut into the last few bars of the music.

"And now we have as our special guest Professor Courtney-Jones from Thames Vale University. Good morning Professor." There was a grunted "Good morning" from Courtney-Jones. "Now Professor, you have been much in the news recently with your theory that lead residues from petrol are harming our children."

Courtney-Jones launched into a tirade against the greedy petroleum companies and their insistence on using tetraethyl lead to enhance the performance of cars without any regard to the growing evidence that lead had a detrimental effect on the growing brains of children. Young tried several times to break in with questions, but Courtney-Jones was determined to present his evidence relating to lead levels in playground dust and the corresponding IQ levels of children in the schools. In the end Young broke in to thank his guest and introduce the next record.

"That man is doing a good job," declared Giuseppe. "We all love the motor car too much!"

"My husband works in the same department as the Professor," Florence told him as he handed her the ham, cheese and pasta. "Excellente," said Giuseppe, while his wife peered at the sleeping Cordelia as she held the shop door open for Florence. "Che bella!" she said again.

★　★　★　★　★

After lunch, Jonas went to find the Research Officer who carried out experiments for Courtney-Jones. This was an historical post from a time when universities had better funding and professors were treated like celebrities. It was not unusual for technicians to clean the professorial cars, carry out small DIY jobs or even relay the asphalt on the tennis court at their country residence. This particular Research Officer, David Pickering by name, had received his BSc first class from Thames Vale University, then stayed on for his PhD study under Courtney-Jones' supervision. He had then been appointed Research Officer. He was far too valuable as a synthetic chemist to be used for mundane occupations, and was kept busy making molecules for further study by the research groups of Courtney-Jones and Albert Greenough. Jonas had been given special leave to ask Pickering to make a key molecule for his research.

Jonas knocked on the door to Pickering's lab office, which was just along the corridor from his own. A grunt from within prompted him to enter the room. On the bench opposite he saw a large glass reaction vessel containing a grey suspension, which was being stirred vigorously in a colourless solvent. From a side arm, a slow trickle of a slightly yellow solution entered the reaction vessel via a stopcock at the base of a pear-shaped glass funnel. As each drop of solution reached the grey suspension there was a burst of effervescence and the solvent boiled up the inside of a vertical condenser before condensing and running back into the reaction vessel.

"Sorry to disturb you when you're busy, but can I leave

this research paper that describes the synthesis I'd like you to do for me?" asked Jonas. "I hope Professor Courtney-Jones mentioned it to you."

Fred Pickering grunted his assent. He was a very earnest man of about forty and lived for his work, rarely leaving his lab office except for a brief sandwich break at lunchtime or a visit to the gents. "The Prof did mention it, but you'll have to wait until I've finished this important work for Dr Lewis" he said.

"That's fine, whenever you're ready. Just give me a buzz and I'll come and discuss the prep with you." Jonas placed the research paper on the desk and left Pickering to get on with his work.

Later Jonas was talking to Albert Greenough in the corridor when they were interrupted by a resounding smashing noise as glass burst out of the window of Fred Pickering's nearby office. The fire and smoke alarms burst into cacophonous life almost instantaneously, and Jonas found himself hard on the heels of Albert Greenough as they both rushed down the corridor to ascertain the cause of the commotion. Black acrid smoke poured out of the lab office as they flung open the door.

"Best leave this to the professionals," coughed Albert as he put down the CO_2 extinguisher he had grabbed from the wall. "Let's get out of here!"

Jonas was only too happy to agree, and they both ran down the two flights of stairs and left the building by the main door. Fortunately it was Wednesday afternoon and there were no undergraduates in the building, but the car park quickly filled with an excited crowd of academic staff, research staff and technicians.

Jonas noticed a very agitated Pickering being comforted by Brian Thatcher, the Chief Technician, and several other colleagues. Within minutes two fire engines and a turntable ladder vehicle tore into the car park and disgorged eager firemen, two of them furiously donning breathing apparatus. These two entered the building, while the turntable ladder was quickly positioned close to the shattered window of Pickering's lab office. A high-pressure stream of water was soon being directed into the office. The pall of smoke changed from black to light grey and then to white, and finally stopped altogether.

Evidently the two firemen with breathing apparatus had now entered the room, because they began throwing items of equipment out of the window. Initially these were items of still-smoking glassware, but they were followed by smouldering furniture and finally, and most spectacularly, an infra-red spectrometer, which curved downwards in a grand arc before disintegrating on impact with the car park.

All those who heard the ear-splitting smash of metal and glass as it hit the tarmac commented on the extraordinary way this old but precision instrument released so many flying parts in an instant. The destruction was all the more significant since this venerable device had been the oldest example of its type still in daily use and bore a certificate from its manufacturer to testify to this fact, a kind of 'blue plaque' of antiquity. All agreed it was a magnificent end for a fine instrument.

The subsequent report by the fire brigade included a statement from Fred Pickering that he had just nipped to the toilet, and that the water supply to his condenser must have switched itself off. This had allowed the hot ether vapours to rise out of the top of the condenser and make contact with the hot heating mantle in which the reaction vessel sat.

Finally the University Safety Officer arrived and ordered everyone to go home and under no circumstances to talk to the press. Probably no one did, but the *Daily Mirror* still carried a short piece the next day under the heading *Boffins in Fireball Terror*.

That evening Florence and Jonas talked about the day's events while they ate their cannelloni stuffed with Parma ham and spinach topped with a tomato sauce. Cordelia had taken her evening feed early, so they had the luxury of a dinner without one of them feeding or winding at the same time. Jonas told her all about the fire and his suspicions that Pickering was making speed for Rob Lewis and John Brewer. Florence mentioned what she had heard on the Jimmy Young show about Courtney-Jones and his anti-lead campaign..

"Courtney-Jones is becoming too famous for my liking" said Jonas. "I had to give one of his lectures again today, a bit of a pain. He's just never around. It's not exactly what I thought I'd be doing."

"But it's all for the good of the environment, surely?"

"Yes, I'm sure he's right, but he's got a hell of a job trying to convince the industrialists and MPs with their vested interests."

Jonas leaned over and gave her a kiss. "The cannelloni was delicious, and I am feeling less stressed, but after the day I've had, I could use a bit of additional de-stressing therapy."

Florence grinned and gave him a knowing look. "I know what you're after, well you'll have to be gentle with me!"

Later as they lay entwined on the sofa, the phone rang and Jonas went to answer it. It was Noel Grimwold. He'd had a call from Courtney-Jones' wife. There had been an accident and Courtney-Jones had spun off the road into a tree. He was badly shaken but had no major injuries. There was some talk of faulty brakes and Noel said that the family were convinced they had been tampered with, though personally he was unconvinced by such conspiracy theories.

Jonas returned to the sofa looking very shaken.

"What's happened?" asked Florence.

"Courtney-Jones had an accident on his way home from seeing the MPs. He's been hurt but he'll be OK."

"Oh God, that's awful."

"It sounds as if there's a chance that his car was tampered with, though the way he drives I'm surprised he doesn't crash into things all the time."

"Jeez, this chemistry's dangerous stuff!"

"You're right. Police on the phone about drug dealers this morning, a bloody great conflagration this afternoon and attempted murder this evening! I was really happy with our new life and it's already coming unravelled. God, if Courtney-

Jones gets himself killed and Rob Lewis gets put in jail, I shall have to do all of their lectures. I've spent all of these years getting a PhD and doing postdoc research for all the right people, and now I'm destined to be a dogsbody."

She put her arms round him and kissed him. "But chemistry isn't everything. We've got a lovely new daughter, a nice house and best of all, you've got back your sexy wife. Who needs chemistry?"

And he knew she was right. Thirty odd years of being an academic stretched ahead of him, plenty of time to make a name for himself, and there was more to life than chemistry. A lot more; two gorgeous girls called Florence and Cordelia for a start. He turned to give Florence a kiss, just as they both heard Cordelia start to cry.

"Back to the real world. I'll go and see if she needs a change" sighed Florence. She headed upstairs while Jonas went to the kitchen to wash the dishes. Life was full of simple pleasures. A lovely wife and daughter, a nice house, good food and wine, wonderful sex. She was right. Who needed chemistry?

ND - #0479 - 270225 - C0 - 234/156/20 - PB - 9781861511065 - Matt Lamination